CONTENTS

I

SYNOPSIS

There are very few novels which have been written about B.A.O.R and even less about The Territorial Army Volunteer Reserve, which on mobilization, would have provided a substantial amount of the total war establishment of 1 British Corps in Germany.

This novel follows one troop of a Yeomanry Armoured Reconnaissance Regiment whilst carrying out its bi-annual deployment during the 1980's. It brings to light, the individual character and background of those who volunteered to serve, and the nature of the duties they performed.

Those who didn't serve or perhaps are only aware of the activities of The Regular Army, might be surprised at the intensity of the deployment, for in two weeks they had to realise the same level of experience and proficiency as that of their Regular Army counterparts.

Hopefully, this account will enlighten some and stir the distant memories of those who served forty years ago, particularly in The Royal Yeomanry and The Queens own Yeomanry.

SPEARPOINT

A NOVEL OF THE COLD WAR

LEE WALKER

INTRODUCTION

Produced out of boredom during COVID and a period of convalescence, this story follows a Yeomanry Armoured Reconnaissance Squadron deploying to Germany in the 1980's. Meant as a bit of fun, hopefully it will appeal to those who had similar experiences, especially with The Royal Yeomanry and Queens Own Yeomanry.

Cheers..

II

THE YEOMANRY

Formed in 1794 as a response to the rise of Republicanism on the continent, The Yeomanry was the mounted faction of a military organisation known as "The Fencibles". Recruited locally, they became a home guard force, responsible for the defence of the country in the absence of The Regular Army. At its height it could boast 206 independent troops but following The Peace of Amien, it was reduced substantially. During the 18th and 19th centuries it served mainly as a police force and was concerned with the social unrest associated with The Luddites and The Chartists, precursors to The Trade Unions. Its' first overseas service commitment was during The South African War. The Boer farmers who were resisting the attentions of The British Empire, fought in a manner which could not be countered by the rigid European battlefield practices of The Regular Army. The attributes of units such as The Yeomanry and Light Horsemen of Australia and New Zealand, with the ability to live off the land and travel light, turned the balance. During The First World War, they were deployed to the Middle East and involved in many police actions as well as Allenby's campaign against The Turkish Empire. They also gave up their mounts to serve as infantry in the ill-conceived campaign at Gallipoli.

In 1939, many Yeomanry Units, still mounted, again returned to The Middle East before converting to Armoured, Artillery and Signals roles. They fought throughout The North African, Sicilian and Italian campaigns, landed on D-Day in Normandy and won many distinctions including being the first British troops to enter Germany. They rated amongst the biggest recipients of Battle Honours in The British Army.

Following the Second World War and with the drawdown from empire, The Territorial Army was greatly reduced in size. The original Regiments were amalgamated and are today represented by The Regiments of The Royal Yeomanry, The Queens Own Yeomanry, The Royal Wessex Yeomanry and The Scottish and North Irish Yeomanry.

For the most part, they still operate in the role of Light Cavalry.

III

AUTUMN FORGE

"Autumn Forge" is the generic name for a series of NATO exercises which were held annually. Their main goal was to practice the mobilization of its' members' armed forces in response to any hostile action taken by The Soviet Union.

Broken into a series of smaller exercises, it involved all three services of each nation and traditionally began once the harvest in Germany had been taken in.

"Spear point" was the name for The British land element of these manoeuvre's and included the deployment of The Territorial Army from The UK.

This is the scenario which sets the backdrop for this novel.

COMPOSITION OF A YEOMANRY ARMOURED RECCONAISANCE SQUADRON

RHQ

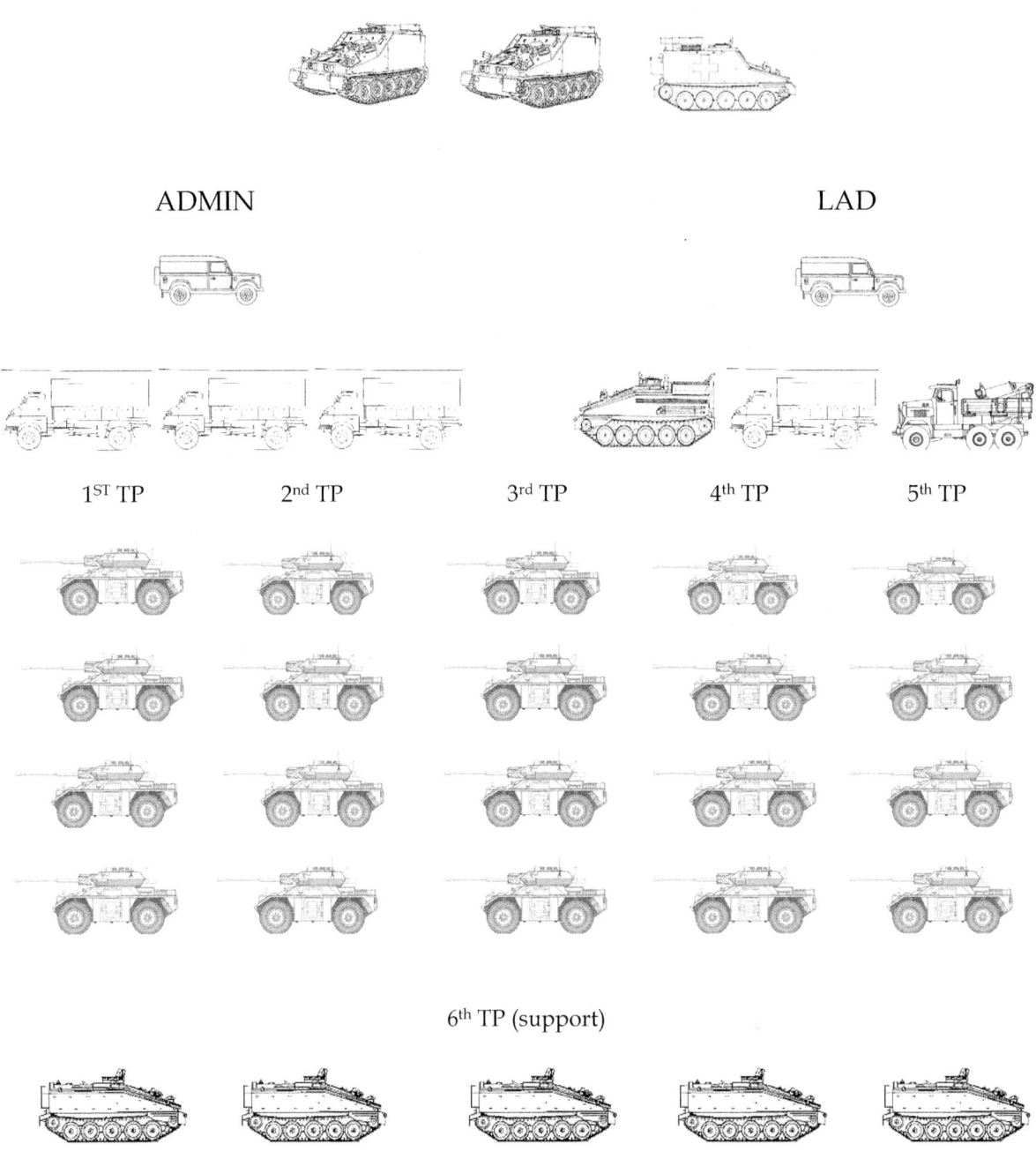

ADMIN

LAD

1ST TP

2nd TP

3rd TP

4th TP

5th TP

6th TP (support)

CHAPTER ONE

DEPLOYMENT

THE PSI

From the mezzanine, Ron Andrews looked down critically onto the floor of the drill hall below him and the sea of bodies, which was a swirl of activity. He observed with a skill born of years of experience, noticing those who were actually working and the inevitable few who were making a good show of doing nothing at all. Picking out the N.C.O's who were conducting the performance, he reflected on his own station in all this. Although a Squadron Sergeant Major in rank, as part of the cadre of Permanent Staff Instructors, his duties were more administrative. He oversaw a team of men who were all regular soldiers as compared to the Territorials below him. Traditionally, Territorial Army units contained a group of men from their parent regiment in The Regular Army, the aim being to provide a continuity of traditions and skills. The post also gave soldiers an opportunity to escape the everyday existence of The Regiment with its discipline and regulations as a member of an armoured unit in B.A.O.R. Each of the Sergeants under him were qualified instructors in driving and maintenance, signals or gunnery the skill and experience of the Territorials though meant that they also had their own equally qualified instructors.

As a "lifer", he had joined straight from school at sixteen, hoping to escape the oppressive atmosphere of having been brought up in the deprived community of a small pit village, which didn't have a pit. Instead of moving away in search of a new life and employment, the inhabitants had remained in the forlorn hope of the mines opening again. Finding it depressing, he couldn't wait to move away. His Father had objected to the notion of him joining The Army, and like so many of his fellow recruits, had his older brother sign the consent forms. Most of his time had been spent in Germany, moving between postings with the occasional tour in Ulster where they guarded The Maze prison or manned vehicle check points. Every three or four years they had the chance to travel to BATUS in Canada. Here, they took part in live fire exercises involving full battle groups, an activity which was impossible on the North German plain, which was now congested with expanding towns and cities. Conservation groups had also greatly reduced the activities of the military, frowning on large scale exercises He was now coming to the end of his career and had opted to take up his present position as a way of transitioning to civilian life. It allowed him time to find employment, buy a house and adjust to his new existence. The "real world" had come as a bit of a shock, The Army not really preparing him for it all. Everyday things like tax and insurance, medical cover and finance had all been taking care of before. Having tried to apply for a mortgage, the broker could not believe that he had no credit history or proof of his existence in The UK. He had tried to explain that he had lived in Germany for the last twenty years in a rented MOD property and that Army regulations plus a minimal wage had prevented taking out large scale credit loans. The broker was also concerned that he had managed to get into The UK without a passport? He had to explain that he had travelled by military aircraft with only his ID card. This lack of knowledge of the military had also been evident in the attitude of employers that he had approached, having never served, unlike their Fathers and Grandfathers. His experience, skill sets and personal attributes were irrelevant, "not much call for a tank driver" was the general consensus of opinion.

This would be his last exercise, in a few months' time, he would be "Dined out" by The Sergeants Mess and the thought filled him with dread. At least it would be a happy time for his wife June. Once he had completed training, got his first foot on the promotion ladder and established himself in The Regiment, his thoughts had turned to a companion to share his new life with. His first tour in Ulster had been a wakeup call and he had reasoned that he needed someone to return to, to justify it all. On his next leave home, they had met, dated, got engaged and he had dragged her off to Germany with stories of overseas travel, subsidized fully furnished houses and a new life. Respectfully, she had accepted the reality of life as a "camp follower" well. She had had to endure living in a foreign country, separated from her family and friends, living in a house which was furnished by The Army and had to be kept to a strict standard of cleanliness. The other wives also enforced a class system which dictated who you could associate with dependent on their husbands' rank. For much of the time, she was left alone to run the house and bring up the kids while he was overseas or on courses. Later on the kids had gone off to boarding school before starting their own separate lives. It was a strange reality that, as often happened, both of his sons had joined The Army and his Daughter had married a soldier. For the first time in her life, June had her own home, which she could furnish and decorate as she felt fit. She would never have to move again or be separated from her husband. The kids had gone but she had the grandkids to look forward to.

Ron looked to the future with uncertainty, his thoughts returning to what the next two weeks would hold for him.

THE TROOP LEADER

To an outsider it would look like chaos, but Lt Stewart Charlesworth recognized it as a controlled chaos. It was the fourth time this year that the squadron had gone through this performance, mobilizing for yet another exercise, some wondering if they would ever have to do it for real. In one corner of the drill hall, men were queuing to sign out their sleeping bags and liners, the vehicle commanders also drawing compasses, batteries, torches, watches, china graph pens and a host of other items that they would need to perform their roles. In the opposite corner, others queued at the armoury for their personal weapons. The vehicle gunners grumbling that they also had to draw the co-axial GPMG's and cleaning kits. The crew's personal weapon was the SMG, a descendant of the World War 2 Sten, it was very basic in construction. The guys liked them because they were small and light and could be stored anywhere on the wagons. They were also "squaddie proof" and could be kicked about in the bottom of a turret without damaging them. On the minus side, they were known to discharge if dropped and useless beyond a range of twenty meters. It was joked that if you wanted to clear a room, you only had to chuck it inside and close the door, it would do the job for you. The magazine was also a perfect bottle opener.

Stewart observed with pride the way his guys handled the weapons and seemed to project an aura of confidence in the way they carried them. This was the culmination of a long year of training, especially for the new soldiers. Starting off with individual training including weapon handling, field craft, first aid and chemical warfare drills, it progressed to trade training and then field exercises. Drills were learnt first at vehicle level, then at troop, squadron and finally regiment. Annual camp allowed all these skills to be put into practice in an intense two week period. Regular Army units had the luxury of being able to practice the various tasks associated with an armoured recce role throughout the year, Territorial units had this one two week period to put it all into practice. Expected to meet the same exacting standards, they often exceeded that of their regular counterparts. FTX's as a part of B.A.O.R. Only occurred, on average, every two or three years with the intervening schemes being held in The UK and consisting of one week of gunnery and one week on a training area with a church parade thrown in. Some people preferred to attend courses instead.

In yet another corner of the hall, soldiers were signing for their I.D. cards and being issued with will forms, should they wish to complete them. They were also being given their dog tags, which had never happened before and raised a few eyebrows amongst the more experienced men. Stewart was a solicitor as had been his Father and Grandfather. Traditionally, the family had taken commissions in The Inns of Court Yeomanry which tended to recruit officers from the legal profession but had lost its armoured role. Educated at Uppingham, as a member of the Combined Cadet Force, he often joined the local Yeomanry Regiment on exercises. It benefitted the unit by boosting numbers and also proved to be a good recruiting ground for both Regular and Territorial Officers. It seemed an obvious choice to take a Reserve Commission and continue to practice law. His elder brother had scoffed at the role and choosing to take a different path, was now a pilot in The Royal Air Force. To his mind the aspects of the two appointments were very different. In The Air Force, as a rule, twenty to thirty airmen were responsible for getting one Officer, (the pilot) into combat. In the Army, a Troop or Platoon leader was responsible for getting twenty to thirty troops into battle, with the correct training, equipment and skills to allow them to perform their role effectively and survive.

Startled from his thoughts, he was aware of a Corporal who smartly saluted him and said "Squadron Leaders compliments Sir, but could all Officers and Sergeants join him in his office Sir"

Stewart caught the attention of his Troop Sergeant who appeared to be giving one of the troop members a "beasting" and they joined the small group leaving the hall.

THE TROOP SERGEANT

"You're from Beeston aren't you? What are they doing now that the village idiot is going to Germany eh? You useless git! See the stores and they might issue you with some more. Hopefully they'll charge you for it".

It was just as well that he had decided to do a kit check on his lads, most of them were pretty solid but one or two weren't worth their rations. George Stafford knew that the outburst had drawn the attention of others, particularly the other Troop Sergeants who viewed the inspection as being unnecessary and typical of him. George knew that his approach to the job was different to the others but then **he** was a different type of character. The only member of the Sergeants Mess who was an ex regular he was also the only one who wasn't a local by birth. It was more of a private members club than a mess with the rest of them having attended the same schools, dated the same girls, known each other all their lives and even brought up their families together. It was a recognized fact that elevation to "the piggery" As the Sergeants Mess was known, was by popular association rather than military skill and competence.

He had served his time in a regular cavalry regiment, his career being pretty typical, with all the usual postings and experiences and he had eventually been promoted to Sergeant. His youngest child had been born with a heart defect and unable to cope alone with the constraints that army life put on them, his wife had begged him to leave and return to civilian life. They had chosen to return to her home town where she would have the support of her family and he had managed to buy into a franchise which gave him a certain amount of self-autonomy. Deep down he resented his predicament and knew that it was reflected in his attitude to other people and often isolated him from them. When he joined this unit he had been forced to drop a rank but had soon re-acquired it and he knew that he perhaps took it all a bit too seriously. It might be a hobby for others, but it was escapism to him and when he went away on schemes, he pushed the real world and all its associated issues to the back of his mind.

He noticed that "The lad" as he tended to think of his Troop Leader, was motioning to him. He was pretty good all said, quietly confident and popular with the lads who called him "Charlie" behind his back, "Boss or Skipper" in private but always "Sir" in company.

As they entered The Squadron Leaders' office he noticed all the other Officers and senior ranks. They consisted of four Sabre Troop Leaders and their Sergeants, the fifth troop being commanded by a Staff Sergeant. The L.A.D. and ADMIN Troops were also run by Staff Sergeants but these were already en-route to Germany, having left with the land party that morning. Support Troop was commanded by an ex regular officer, who having been Infantry, was better suited to their role within The Squadron. The Support Troop was carried in five Spartan APC's and their roles included dismounted OP's, foot patrols, vehicle check points and force protection. They also had the ability to lay or clear mines and use explosives to deny assets to an enemy. Being the biggest of the Troops and considering themselves as something of a private army, they projected a certain arrogance and thought themselves superior to the Sabre Troops. SHQ included The Squadron Leader, Adjutant, two watch officers and a Troop Sergeant.   The O Group covered timings for the intended move to the air head, discussed crew levels within the individual troops and confirmed that all the admin tasks had been completed. The Squadron Leader gave permission for the squadron bar to be opened, if nothing else, to prevent the troops sneaking out to the local. The coaches would depart early the next morning, the first meal being breakfast at Brize Norton.

THE TROOP CORPORAL

Being a Corporal was the best rank as far as Jack Sharp was concerned. Although he was a vehicle commander, he was also still considered to be "one of the boys", still messing, sleeping and socializing with them. If he got any shit from them he could pass it upstairs and if anything came from above he could pass it down. He knew that his face didn't fit and that he would never ascend to The Sergeants Mess, but he was happy with his station in life. As a joke, he always mentioned that Hitler, Napoleon, Idi Amin and Mussolini had all been Corporals. Nobody remembered the Sergeants in history.

Standing with the other Troop Corporal, Pete Wood, he watched the guys packing away their kit following an inspection by George Stafford, the Troop Sergeant. Smudger had let them down again, having failed to show his NBC kit. Jack had provided him with a new suit and was glad that the guy wasn't in his crew. Apart from Pete and George, he was the only member of the Troop who had served in the regulars but the actual details he kept to himself. Only Pete knew the truth.

They had joined The Junior Leaders Regiment R.A.C. at Bovington at the same time and served in Alma troop, A Squadron. Having failed the medical at his first attempt due to poor eyesight, he had applied again later and fooled the drunken medical examiner. However, some months later, his failure to classify on the range had resulted in him being sent to the medical centre. He had managed to qualify on the SMG and pistol purely by natural instinct, but the LMG and Charlie G were right handed weapon systems. He only had partial vision in the right eye. The RSM had wanted to discharge him for Illegal Enlistment as he had basically lied about having tried to join previously. The Commander of The Training Regiment however sympathized with his desire to serve and recognized that he could have been an asset to The Army. He changed the charge to D.A.O.R (Discharged as of right). Returning home as a failure, in his own eyes, nothing in his life would alleviate his disappointment. Trying for the local TA unit, the fact that he already had an army number had meant that the recruitment team had failed to follow the correct procedure. He was fast tracked into the unit, bypassing a recruit course at Catterick and soon established himself. Having served his time, Pete Wood had joined the same unit and kept the secret.

So far he had managed to avoid any scrutiny, being able to classify on the range every year. On his gunnery course, they had qualified on a laser simulator rather than with live weapons and when commanding shoots on the ranges he had been able to get by. His hearing was also failing and he struggled to hear conversations. People assumed his lack of interest in the things that occurred around him was down to a personality trait, unaware of the real cause. In fact, of everyone in the Troop he thought that he was probably the most eligible as a soldier, having been born into a military family, lived on garrisons all over the world and had an intimate knowledge of everything military.

As everyone started to move to the squadron bar he addressed the Troop. "Windy, Jim, you're on first stag, stay with the kit. Briggsy, Paddy, you'll take over in one hour, Frank and Bomber next, then Smudge and Nick". He received the usual retorts but knew that they could be trusted. It was easier to divide it on a crew basis he reasoned.

Pete and he would be last on stag and available to kick them all awake when the time came.

THE TROOPER

Trooper Dave Smith, Smudger to his mates, was still smarting from the "beasting" he had received from his Troop Sergeant. He didn't take it personally, he never did, knowing that his supposedly laid back character left him open to such attention.

It wasn't intentional, he wished that he could stay under the radar and not get noticed. Ever since school he had been unable to apply himself to anything. He had failed at school and later at more than a few jobs having the attention span of a five year old, he just couldn't retain information or concentrate on specific tasks. His Nan had told him when he was a kid that he was moonstruck. His crew mate Nick had suggested that he might be epileptic or mildly autistic. His head just seemed to be full of information all the time which he couldn't control or organise.

He had married and then had kids at a young age. Unable to cope or deal with fatherhood, his wife had quickly grown tired of him. He needed an escape and a friend had told him of The T.A. He liked engines and this unit gave him a chance to tinker with them, socialise and escape his marriage.

They were a good bunch of lads, who seemed to accept him.

Knowing what the squadron bar was going to be like, Pete and Jack, using the cover of darkness, vaulted over the small fence into an adjoining graveyard and out onto the road. After about ten minutes they entered THE CASTLE and scanned the room. They immediately caught the attention of the bar. In the decade of big hair and big shoulder pads, duty was a four letter word and shiny boots and short hair marked you as either police or army. At a corner table sat a group of "old timers" who, alone in the room, raised their pints in salute. Pete and Jack tilted their heads in recognition, Pete noticing that they were all sat facing the exits. A sure sign of past experiences. They chatted about their home and work lives for about two minutes before automatically dropping into talking "shop". Discussing the merits of the guys in the troop and the prospect of the next two weeks, the conversation eventually became more serious. They had both noticed the issue of dog tags earlier, something which didn't usually happen. Recent world events had also become apparent as well. The East Germans had misinterpreted one part of the annual "AUTUMN FORGE" exercises, "ABLE ARCHER", as an actual deployment of tactical nuclear weapons by the Americans into West Germany. They had started their own series of exercises in response. The Soviets were paranoid about any military escalation on their borders.

Also, a Russian "TYPHOON" class nuclear submarine had surfaced off the eastern seaboard of The United States, its presence until then unknown. Arseholes were getting twitchy and **they** were about to deploy to exactly where it would all kick off.

After a couple of hours they returned covertly to the drill hall raising a barrage of ribald remarks from the already drunk occupants on entry.

"Where you two bin then ya dorty bastards"?

"What's your name, Den Hardy"? Came from another, raising a chorus of laughs. Den Hardy was a notorious former member of the unit who had a habit of visiting the wives of soldiers when away from home. He had come to a sticky end.

Pete could also hear the usual comments on such gatherings where people weren't seen from one year to the next.

"Bloody hell, I thought you were dead" and "Fucking hell, is it Bounty Day again"? This harked back to the days when Territorials would receive their annual training bounty of a tax free sum of money. It was issued in cash following the age old ritual of a pay parade. This had led to a score of outrageous stories including drink and dirty women and someone who didn't go home for three days.

There would be some bad heads tomorrow thought Jack.

By ten o'clock The S.S.M. had decided to knock things on the head and ordered the bar shut. He knew that some of the guys would have come straight from work and wouldn't have eaten all day, drink on empty stomachs made for badly behaved soldiers. Some were already pissed and they had a long day ahead of them.

It seemed like they had only just climbed into their sleeping bags when they were woken up again and told to fall in under the scrutiny of The O.C. and S.S.M.

"Some very sick looking soldiers here Sar'nt Major" commented the O.C.

"Yes Sir" came the reply.

The solution was inevitable, formed up outside in the damp mist, The Squadron was run until enough men had thrown up to satisfy his indignation. Within an hour they had sorted themselves out and were boarding the coaches to take them to the Air Movements Centre at Brize Norton. Those who knew tried to get back to sleep, concealing themselves under their jackets. They were more than aware that if they fell asleep with their faces exposed that it would result in them waking up covered in china graph. There was also the old Army words of wisdom "Don't fall asleep with your mouth open or you'll wake up with fifty pence in your hand and a salty taste in your mouth". Some had of course managed to sneak a few bottles of beer on board and these would become much desired items later when the urge came to take a piss. At Brize, they were processed and finally given a meal before a team of men were volunteered to act as a baggage party. These guys loaded The Squadron's gear onto a four tonner which carried them out to the plane, a RAF VC 10. On boarding, Pete noticed that the seats all faced rearwards. This was supposedly to improve the chance of survival following an air crash. It was something which was peculiar to this aircraft in RAF service.

Within a couple of hours of boarding they had landed at Hannover. While they were processed through the terminal and onto more coaches, the baggage party did its thing again. The whole convoy made the one hour road journey to the railway marshalling yards at Brunswick where they found that the Squadron's vehicles had already been unloaded from the freight containers that they had travelled in, presumably by the regimental advance party? Two weeks before, after preparation, they had been driven to a local container depot for shipment to Germany. Part of the team that moved them stayed behind to first guard them and then load those, two per shipment container. As well as full vehicle kits, spare pieces of personal items were locked inside storage bins and other comforts such as alcohol and tobacco. Army vehicles came with standard padlocks with only a few key combinations and so the crews provided their own. Their first priority now was to check that they were secure. The process of preparing them for use started in earnest. Once the drivers had performed the pre-start checks and left them to idle, they set up the BV and started to brew some tea. (The BV was a boiling vessel which was wired into the power supply, fitted with a tap it could provide constant hot water or be used as a pressure cooker. Every modern British Army vehicle had one. In later years it would be acknowledged as "The single piece of kit that won The Cold War". They then sorted out the storage, moving the slave lead and kinetic towrope to drape them over the front of the wagons. When they were first built, the wagons came with a flotation screen and two fiberglass tanks on either side between the wheel stations. These were later modified with large doors to provide excellent storage. One side was "dirty" and used for the oils and tool kits, the other was "clean" and held sleeping bags and personal kit. The crews' webbing was hung on the outside of the wagon. The original rear turret bustle wasn't big enough for the job and most crews replaced them with the rear hull storage bin used on CVR(T)'s. These held all the engine sheets, camouflage nets and rolls of urban camouflage. The walkways running down either side of the vehicle allowed crews to bolt on old shell boxes to provide storage for gas cookers, plates, utensils, food and toiletries. One would hold the personal washing and shaving kits which were kept in the bags which the crews' helmets came in. This made them easy to access and put away again without disturbing other stored items. Some of the kitchens were works of art. There was also storage for two plastic "jerry cans" behind the rear wheels which were used for water and convenient recesses either side of the side bins which were used as dustbins. Some wagons also had toilet seats with folding legs complete with toilet roll holders. The storage space was one of the things which the crews liked, its poor off road performance and "clockwork gun" let it down though.

FOX, like all British Army vehicles was built for export but poor sales meant that it was available to replace The Saladin range of wheeled armoured reconnaissance vehicles in Territorial Army service. Apart from The Household Cavalry and Berlin Brigade, it was only used by the regular infantry battalions of The 2nd Infantry Division. Two TA regiments, The Royal Yeomanry and the Queens Own Yeomanry were the biggest users, operating 80 vehicles each. With a high road speed, large fuel tank and extensive storage, it was able to operate unsupported for a number of days and so was ideal for covering the vast areas involved in rear area security missions. Besides the drivers, the turret crews also had tasks including checking and tuning the radios, mounting the co-axial weapons and storing all the items needed for communications and navigation. Most of the commanders had a "Battle Box", a 7.62mm ammunition box which held torches, batteries, china graph markers, compasses and protractors and the contents were unique to each one.

From his turret Jack looked at the mass of vehicles concentrated here, the regiment could boast perhaps 130 armoured and 160 soft skin vehicles. It was an impressive sight.

On the other side of the boundary road was the sprawling site of a Bundeswehr camp and in the distance he could see a collection of houses and flats. This, he knew, was Kopernickus Strasse. He had lived there when his dad was posted here in the early 70's before they had moved to nearby Wolfenbuttel. They were due to spend their last few days there at Northampton Barracks at the end of this exercise.

From the window of the site office above the marshalling yard, "Casey Jones" looked at the spectacle below him, he wasn't impressed. His real name was Carl Zeigler but he was known as "Casey Jones" by the present generation of kids who worked in the yards, because of his age and his constant stories of driving steam trains. He had started working here in 1941 as a sixteen year old labourer, but due to a high attrition rate, he was quickly promoted to first fireman and then driver. He had lost three engines during the war, one to Russian partisans and another two to allied aircraft in Normandy. He still proudly wore the ribbons of The War Service medal and Iron Cross 2nd Class on his uniform jacket. 1941, now that had been an impressive sight, when Hitler had decided to take his armies East into Russia. Of the 41 boys who had graduated from school with him, he was the last. What a waste, and now they were preparing for another war.

Drinking the brew offered to him by Nick Shields, his driver, Pete was thinking of his own ghosts. When he had passed out from The Junior Leaders at Bovvy, he had joined his regiment at Fallinbostel. His very first exercise with them had been on the Luneberg Heath training area. Throughout that week he kept getting feelings of "de ja vou ". As they travelled around the area it all felt very familiar to him. He instinctively knew what was around each corner and what the next feature would be, although he had never been there before. One night they had moved into a wooded location which had a series of large, long walls in the centre of it.

"What the fuck are these?" his mate had asked. "Ships" he had replied. "Fuck off, we're 60 miles from the sea"
The next day one of the range wardens appeared and the question was put to him. "When we were preparing for the invasion of England, these concrete landing craft were built here to practice loading and offloading tanks" he had replied, "and then when the Allied invasion of Europe was expected, they were used by The Luftwaffe as targets."

This was just one of a few similar experiences he had endured throughout his time in Germany.

As the troop was wading into a brew and some "egg banjos", Charlie returned from an O Group and told them what was going to happen next.

"Starting at 16:00 hours, The Regiment will be executing a road march, in Squadron packets, to Hameln. A Squadron will be leading. We will be escorted by the local autobahn police unit, with no stops. Normal convoy rules will be in force, watch your speed and distance. If you break down you will display a red flag."

"Order of march will be SHQ, then each troop in numerical order with the Samaritan and Samson bringing up the rear. The Regiment must be firm at Hameln by 24:00 tonight. Hopefully we will join the L.A.D. and ADMIN there. We are now on 10 minutes notice to move, any questions?"

"I suggest that drivers do a "first parade" now and start their engines so that we have no surprises" came the professional response from George Stafford.

The crews mounted up and settled down. The old army adage of "Hurry up and wait" came to Pete's mind.

At 16:00 with typical German precision, the move began.

CHAPTER TWO

THE ROAD MARCH

Thirty minutes later the convoy was passing Hildesheim and George was admiring the way that the police were conducting the move. There had been no changes of speed and at the approach of each junction, outriders had sped ahead to close them. The local car drivers seemed to take it all in their stride and pedestrians carried on without paying them any attention. After 40 years of military occupation, this was the norm. The older generation who remembered the war years and the behaviour of The Russian troops as they entered Germany, accepted the presence of The Allies, but the wind was changing and the younger generation resented that presence as well as the large amount of disruption and damage these exercises caused. The country had changed since he had first come out here. The towns and cities had spread in area and the population had grown with the influx of foreign labour. The North German Plain no longer existed. 20 years before it had stretched uninterrupted from Berlin to The Rhine. If The Soviets had come over the border then, they would have "Blitzkrieged" across Upper Saxony. Now, huge cities like Hildesheim Hannover and Brunswick blocked the intended route of The 3rd Shock Army. They would not be able to bypass them and would prove costly to clear. There was also villages and hamlets every quarter of a mile joined by straight roads lined with irrigation ditches and mature trees. Having learnt their lessons in the last war, each community had its' own Volksturm unit, local volunteers with military training and armed with mines, the deadly Milan anti-tank system and Spandaus. The distances between the villages and farms allowed for interlocking fields of fire and combined with their knowledge of the local area, would provide a certain amount of resistance. Also, all new road bridges had been constructed with sealed chambers where shaped charges could be placed to destroy them. The German terrain south of here would prove to be even harder to advance across even though the shortest route to The Rhine was via The Fulda Gap in the American zone. No, he believed that The Soviets had missed their chance and with the political changes in Eastern Europe combined with the mistake of annexing Afghanistan, They would never come west.

As they crossed The Weser, childhood memories again clouded Jacks' thoughts.

The story of "The Pied Piper" was known throughout the world and was Hameln's' biggest tourist attraction. During the summer the people would stage a re-enactment of the story on the steps of the town hall. Kids from local schools would dress up and play the part of the children and the rats in the story. One year, as an act of solidarity, children of the local British Forces School were invited to take part, in the part of the rats of course.

He remembered it with fondness, and the local legends associated with the story. In the middle of the river were a number of islands, one of which had a flax mill. This had to be abandoned when it became infested with rats, the survivors of the cull. The story was still part of local folklore.

Jack woke from his thoughts as they entered Bindon Barracks and parked on the huge and now empty area of concrete which usually housed the bridge trains of the resident Royal Engineer Unit. In The British zone there existed two rivers running north to south, The Weser and The Leine. They formed natural barriers to any Soviet movement from the east and so the ability to either construct bridges or deny them to an enemy was a huge part of both armies' tactical thinking. This was the obvious location for the bridging units who must have been already deployed.

Almost at once, the drivers began their "halt parades", checking external storage and wheel stations for either oil leaks or overheating. The gunners knew their drills as well and were making their way across to the 4 tonners of the ADMIN troop with their shopping lists. Although each vehicle was carrying plenty of issue compo rations, the guys preferred to eat fresh rations in the field. The good stuff would be kept of course but the crap, like tins of rice, margarine and the so called chicken supreme were used to barter with the infantry in exchange for pyro. Traditionally, they had food to spare whereas the infantry carried very little. Likewise they were issued with lots of flares, blank ammo and thunder flashes but the cavalry weren't. It was a good deal for both parties. As a side-line, like most quartermasters in The British Army, this one also supplied beer, fresh meat and tobacco, at a price of course. It was no accident that he was known in the squadron as "Mr 10 percent". The preferred beverage in B.A.O.R. was Herforder Pils which came in easily recognisable yellow cases known universally as "Yellow handbags". The lads tended to go native in their tastes when over there, drinking German beer and eating German food like Bratwurst and Frickadella's, which were traditionally made of horse meat, and Metwurst which was cured mince seasoned with herbs and eaten raw. Within 10 minutes of arriving, The Squadron leader was holding an O group. When Charlie was summoned, he told his gunner, Jim Hardy, to accompany him and bring their map. His job would be to copy the map trace in the CV which would then be transferred to the other vehicle commanders' maps when they returned. He only copied the information that related to his own troops' area of responsibility and details of the two units to the left and right. This would deny information to an enemy should they be captured. Jim remembered that at a talk given by a member of The Intelligence Corps, they had been told that Soviet policy was to only interrogate officers at company or squadron level or above, lesser mortals would be executed. Given that the modern form of battle was very fluid, any information acquired was only good for twenty four hours. The conclusion of course was that interrogation would be efficient and very physical. He had looked at the officers in the room with sympathy. Only three things worried him about going into action, being maimed, failing his mates and being tortured.

When he had finished the trace, he stood with the others and listened as the briefing began. "From this location, the regiment will move to form an O.P. line along the length of the obvious feature running parallel to and between The Leine and The Weser." He indicated his instructions on a laminated wall map, pointing out the features and obstacles as he proceeded. "The route of the approach march will be as follows, from this location we will travel south on the B83 to Emmerthal, the first check point and pick up the L431 west to cross The HamelschenBurg Forest via Welsede, Lowensen, Ludge, Elbrixen, Rischenau, Lowendorf, Bodexen and Albaxen before crossing The Weser at Holzminden. This will be the release point. From here, the Squadrons will move into their individual areas of responsibility. A squadron, with the exception of the L.A.D and ADMIN, will R.V. at this farm complex to the west of Eschershausen once this phase has ended. As we are the lead squadron, we will police the route and establish vehicle check points at junctions along it with callsigns deploying as they reach them. The VCP's have been allocated by troop in alphanumerical order. There are 12 VCP's to be manned by 1st, 2nd and 3rd Troops. This will also be the order of march." Charlie noted that the regiment would be executing a wide sweep first west, south and then east before crossing the river. As 1st Troop of A Squadron they would be leading the move.

"Radio silence will be enforced throughout, the regimental L.A.D will sweep the route for casualties. The whole regiment must be firm in its forward positions by first light, the local authorities will not allow any military vehicle movement tomorrow during daylight hours".

"There are other stipulations that have been issued by the local administration involving the environmental impact of this exercise. There will be no digging of latrines, "porta loos" have been supplied and placed in those positions most likely to be chosen as hides and harbour areas. They are bright yellow in colour and illuminated at night which makes the business of concealment pretty pointless, but you will do so as per normal. Also, within the forests you will notice large conical ant hills about 6 foot in height. These have been introduced to eliminate the parasites which are killing the trees. Do not damage them! The Green Party is growing in power in The German parliament at the moment and flexing its' muscles so we have to appease them".

"One last stipulation, there will be no cutting of Live cam. Dead vegetation and windfall can be used but other than that you will have to rely on cam nets, The Squadron will move at 24:00 hours"

The Squadron Leader looked around at his officers, paused and then nodded to his driver who emerged from the shadows. He was carrying a silver tray with matching stirrup cups arrayed on it which were offered to the attending officers.

"Cornet Hulme, a toast if you please", he addressed the junior officer present who Jim noticed, only looked about 12.

"Gentlemen, I give you, todays Fox".

They replied in chorus and downed the liqueur. Jim smiled inwardly to himself accepting the traditions and eccentricities that were the norm in Cavalry Regiments. Harking back to the days when officers "rode to hounds" even when on campaign. It was still trendy for them to own ugly dogs with silly names.

He followed Charlie back to the troop where the details were copied from his map and the orders repeated. Charlie liked to keep everyone in the troop "in the loop" but George resented the fact that as Troop Sergeant he should be included more in the decision making. In his eyes there might come a time when he was excluded from voicing an opinion on a subject which could result in the troop being put in harm's way.

As they waited for the move, they prepared the vehicles and their personal equipment for a night operation.

Turning out of the gates, Charlie led the Troop south along the bank of the Weser. Within 5 minutes he had reached the exit for Emmerthal and he pulled over at the junction at the top of the exit road allowing the rest of the troop to pass.

He only just had time to re-position so that he was facing the direction of travel when the next Troop arrived, Jim Hardy rushed across to act as point's man, switching on the "lollipop" as he went. Luckily he had kitted up with his webbing and weapon before leaving the barracks. The "lollipop" was exactly that, with a red lens on one side and a green one on the other which could be illuminated and used for traffic control. The passing crews gave him the expected verbal abuse as he ran across the road. He realised that the dark camouflage clothing he wore wasn't much use in this situation and that he was fair game for any local rushing home from the pub.

A couple of miles further on, George Stafford pulled over. His waypoint was a T junction and easy to police, Briggsy moved into position and he told Paddy to get a "brew" on

On the other side of a railway bridge, within sight of George, was the next waypoint, a Y shaped junction this time which would need to be manned by two people. With only one "lollipop", Bomber, the driver, had to use a torch.

When Pete's wagon reached their checkpoint they couldn't believe their luck. Situated at a junction opposite the railway station at Bad Pyrmont, directly opposite them was a "Schnelle". Schnelle Imbis was a franchise of fast food stalls which were prolific all over Germany, selling hot take - a - way food and Fries with everything. Pete tapped Smudger on the head and announced, "Your round mate, 3 currywurst with fries, Nick, you're on stag".

As the rest of the squadron passed by, many of them mouthed the word "Bastard" to Pete and his crew, he hoped that Nick would get back before SHQ and "The Boss" appeared.

It didn't take long for the four squadrons to pass Charlie's position as HQ Squadron and all the road parties which had driven from England would remain at Hameln over the weekend. RHQ made its own way to a local high point where it would have radio coverage for the next stage of the exercise. Collecting the other crews as he passed by, Charlie moved into Bad Pyrmont, realising with disgust that the "Schnelle" was now closed. Pete and his crew made a great show of enjoying their meals and received a round of abuse in return.

As they moved to the bridge at Holzminden, the troop fell in behind the rest of the squadron as it passed, like a snake uncoiling itself. After crossing the river, the squadron travelled North East for ten miles along the floor of a valley with forested hills on either side. At this point the valley turned South East with the village of Eschershausen at its neck. On the western side of the village sat a large farm complex and digester plant. This was SHQ's hide location and the rally point for the next phase. As the vehicles turned into it and off the main road, the drivers flicked their blackout switches on. Thankfully there was guys on the ground who guided them by shielded torchlight into position. Once the whole squadron had arrived, the individual troops began to move to their O.P. locations, aware that they had to be firm by sunrise. It had been a long 24 hours since leaving the drill hall and it wasn't over yet

CHAPTER THREE

THE O.P. LINE

Eschershausen lay in a bowl with three valleys running South West, North West and South East from it. These were lined with wood covered ridges. On the north east side of the town, the ridge, known as the Grunenplan, ran parallel to a second lower one with a shallow valley of farmland in between. Behind that second ridge lay the River Leine and the town of Alfeld. These two ridges were crossed by three roads which met at Eschershausen before continuing south west to The River Weser at Holzminden. Combined together, the two rivers and two ridgelines formed a succession of obstacles which a Soviet army invading from East Germany would have to cross. This was the scene for the exercise. The Grunenplan ridge provide an elevated O.P. line covering the three roads approaching from the east and was manned by a Yeomanry Armoured Reconnaissance Regiment. The part of the enemy was being played by elements of a German Panzer Grenadier Brigade. The three roads were covered from north to south by 2nd, 1st and 3rd Troops with 4th Troop covering the open end of the main valley to the south east. 5th Troop was held in reserve in Eschershausen along with SHQ consisting of 2 Sultans (armoured command vehicles), the Samaritan (armoured ambulance), the Samson (armoured recovery vehicle), a Ferret (armoured liaison vehicle) and 2 Spartans (armoured personnel carriers), whose sections were to provide force protection.

The 3 other Spartans of Support Troop were deployed on the main road to Alfeld where it crossed the spine of The Grunenplan ridge.

1st Troop were to establish an O.P. on the forward slope of The Grunenplan Ridge covering the road which ran directly from Alfeld. To its left was 2nd Troop and to its right 3rd with their own arcs of responsibility. The Grunenplan forest was crisscrossed with a pattern of trails which allowed the troop to approach undetected with the lights blacked out. Just short of the forward edge they halted and Charlie went forward on foot. Once again George felt that he wasn't being included and looked at their position on the map. They appeared to be in a shallow bowl within the forest with the track they had come up leading back to a junction which would allow them to traverse the whole length of the ridge if necessary.

As he approached the forward edge of the wood, it became obvious to Charlie that the lack of foliage would prevent them using one of the wagons as a mounted O.P. It would have to consist of a dismounted team in a camouflaged hide with a radio landline leading back to the vehicles. They would also use one of the drivers' night sights on a ground mount to provide night vision. The command cable and ground mounting were not standard issue and had been fabricated by the squadron fitters at his request. The idea had been a suggestion of Pete Woods' which Charlie had taken on board.

Returning to the troop he laid out his plan.

"The forward edge of the forest is about 100 meters ahead. As you can see about you, there is no ground cover or foliage so it will have to be a dismounted O.P. Sunrise is 08:45 it is now 06:00. The O.P. has to be up and running by 08:00 so that is the priority, Sar'nt Stafford and Corporal Sharp will assist me to get it established. Corporal Wood, (he indicated him by a nod of the head), you will set up the vehicle hide here and arrange a stag for sentry duty. Keep it simple with as little noise as possible, we have all day to get straight".

"Yes boss" he replied, his mind already two jumps ahead.

"You all know the drills, so crack on, the sooner it's done the sooner we can all get some shuteye".

"Boss, yes boss, right skipper" came a selection of responses.

Pausing to take breath, he continued…

"If the position is approached or compromised you will mount up and prepare to defend it. If we are forced to crash out, the primary R.V. is the first junction along the track we came in by. The troop will wait there for 15 minutes before moving to the secondary R.V, the next junction, for a further 15 minutes".

"If you miss both R.V's, follow the Woodline back up the valley to Eschershausen and SHQ's location. Today's passwords are, a nice easy one to remember this…the challenge is ALPHA BRAVO and the response is BRAVO ALPHA. Just think of The Swedish pop group. Any questions? Carry on".

The O.P. team returned to the forward edge of the forest and squatting against the bases of three trees, faced each other and discussed the job at hand.

"We can't use the cam nets as there is no other foliage and digging will be a bastard because of the overlapping tree roots" George commented. This was a managed forest, the trees having been planted in neat lines to assist in harvesting.

"I'd prefer to stay away from these bloody termite nests as well" Charlie replied.

Jack intervened…

"If we use the hessian, it's a similar colour to the ground and make do with a shallow shell scrape with a few of the cut logs that have been left, we'll be laid down, it won't be very comfortable and we will have to crawl in and out of it, but it might work?"

George and Charlie nodded in agreement. The troop was carrying three different sets of camouflage, the traditional two tone green cam nets, white tarpaulin and rolls of hessian painted on one side to look like brickwork. The decision to bring the white tarpaulin came from the knowledge that German farmers had a tendency to use it to cover piles of straw, wood and machinery. There was nothing easier than to throw it over the wagons and it made an instant waterproof shelter. The rolls of hessian painted to look like walls were wrapped around the vehicles and an engine sheet pitched to look like a roof. This had come about following a change in tactical thinking. In the 1950's and 60's vehicles would hide in villages, barns and farms but these were considered to be vulnerable. They were marked on maps and made easy reference points for artillery and so the use of woods and forests was encouraged. The 70's saw the introduction of thermal imagers, tank engines took hours to cool down and it was impossible to hide the thermal signatures of exposed features like hands and faces. So now they had reverted to using buildings which heated up during the day and concealed the heat signatures.

When the guys were told to paint the hessian, they took it as the usual sort of bullshit idea that some staff officer had come up with. Some comedians had to rip the arse out of it as usual, adding doors and windows with flowerpots in them. One crew even added milk bottles on the front step and a cat sat in the window. If they used the unpainted side though, it would blend in with the sandy ground and tree trunks.

It was decided that Jack would bring the hessian and shovels, George the night sight and telephone and Charlie the maps torches and paraphernalia needed for the O.P. Once the hide was constructed, they laid the command wires and returned to the vehicles to sort out the details of timings, crews and duty's.

Pete had positioned the four vehicles in a fan shape within the bowl with their fronts facing the exit track. The wagons already had the personal cam added at Hameln, pre-cut so as to drape over the turrets and hulls without blocking the hatches. It was only two hours until daylight when they could complete the hide making the least possible noise and he told the lads to get their heads down where they could with their personal weapons and gas respirators at hand. Everyone was knackered and there was no argument.

He decided to use his own crew as guard for now, positioning Smudger 100 meters down the track and Nick on the rear rim of the bowl where he could cover all the approaches. He would himself stay awake though until the O.P. team returned. The routine would start at 08:00 two hours on and four hours off. The plan involved folding his own crew into the three others providing three teams of four, two guys in the O.P. one sentry on the track and the fourth up-wind where he could cover the hide and also act as NBC sentry. He would have full protective gear on, the chemical detector and a rattle to signal any alarm.

The rattle was exactly that, used at football matches for generations, it had been utilized in the trenches during The First World War to signal a gas attack. It was practical and much more reliable than a klaxon or siren.

When it was light enough to see, he woke the crews and they set about building garages around the wagons with the cam nets which they could quickly exit if necessary. They also put up the bivvies, again, where they would not obstruct the wagons. He decided to use only three of them as there was three teams now. This would prevent the disruption caused by people returning to their own vehicle bivvies. The teams would sleep, eat and work separately. The other wagons were conspicuous in their green camouflage.

He had sought out some old nets at an army surplus store which were made of hemp and brown hessian strips and blended in better with the brown/red hues of the tree trunks and forest floor. Modern nets were two tone green, plastic and supposedly coated with a chemical which reflected radiation although he didn't believe it. Being down in the bowl though, detection from above was the only issue.

On their return The Boss and George seemed happy with his work, especially the stag system which they had expected to have to set up themselves. He had also advised the guys who were about to go on stag, that when they cooked, they prepare sandwiches and a flask of tea for the O.P. teams.

By 08:00 everything was in place and "stand to" was carried out from 08:15 until 09:15 with everyone except those on duty mounted up. With the daylight, Pete was able to take a walk around the area. The only concealed approach to the hide was along what looked like a drainage ditch which he decided to cover with a tripwire and flare. Whilst setting it up later he became aware of a strong ammonia smell and found evidence of a family of wild boar who were rutting under a fallen tree. One of them had a shock of red hair which gave him the appearance of a punk rocker. They were fiercely territorial animals who he knew would have set trails through the forest.

These were easy to find and he noticed that they didn't come near the hide site, probably because of the constant presence of humans there? Earlier on he had found evidence of other occupants, clips of blank ammo and discarded ration boxes.

In the O.P. Charlie had finally got himself organised and with the improving light started to make out a range card. This was a chart with a concentric arc of lines. The base of the arc represented his own position and drawing features he could see on to the chart, calculated bearings and distance to them. Centre of arc was, of course, the gap in the ridgeline where the main road carried traffic across the valley but he also recorded features which could provide hide areas or covered approaches to the O.P. He had purposefully taken first watch so that he could do this and was pleased that the position they had chosen in the dark, would not have to be moved now that it was light. The fact that there was evidence of previous use had not escaped him though and he wondered how many others had used this spot?

Cpl Wood had reminded him that the wagon which the night sight and radio where connected to would have to be started every hour to recharge the batteries. He seemed to have a natural skill for recognising details which others missed. Quiet and unassuming he had an aura of professionalism about him which intrigued Charlie.

As the light improved he started to notice different things, particularly the hundreds of Hares which appeared in the middle of the ploughed fields, as if by magic. Some were huge things, well over two foot high and went some way to explaining the shooting towers which lined the tree line. They already knew that there would be no movement before midnight tonight and Charlie wondered if he would be able to stay awake throughout his watch. Jim Hardy was already drifting in and out of sleep beside him and they still had another hour to go. At 14:00 hrs Charlie was back in the O.P. again. He could hardly believe that he had just had 4 hours sleep, a wash and something to eat. Despite the ban on vehicle movement there had still been activity throughout the day.

One of the little German BO 105 observation helicopters had just passed up the valley parallel with the tree line. This had been happening all day, its purpose unknown. It didn't seem to have any cameras or sights on it. There had been no other obvious activity except for the now familiar humming noise and a shadow quickly crossing the valley. This was one of the many gliders seen that day. Along the top of the ridge behind them were a number of gliding fields, there was no thermal activity but the ridge soaring was obviously good here?

Out of the corner of his eye he spied something bright and lifted his binoculars to scrutinize it. Coming through the gap in the opposite tree lined ridge was a bright yellow and silver artic with what looked like Polish advertising on the side. He followed it for a few seconds more before losing interest and eating the oatmeal block topped with cheese and jam offered up by Jim Hardy. The tin that the cheese came in was marked "Cheese processed" but was universally known as "Cheese possessed" because of the hallucinations some guys had if they ate too much of it. Charlie quite liked it and thought that it tasted a bit like Austrian smoked. The bottle of Herforder he washed it down with was also very welcome and he settled in for the rest of the stag.

The yellow and silver artic was indeed Polish but its driver was a Sergeant in The Polish Special Forces who had made this trip to The Rhine six times now. As they crossed the shallow valley he looked at the distant tree line knowingly and understood why the German helicopter was behaving in the manner it was. The man in the passenger seat looked like any other East European co-driver but he was in fact the Battalion Commander of a Soviet Motor Rifle unit. Newly arrived at his unit stationed just outside Magdeburg, he was making a covert reconnaissance of the route his Battalion would have to take to carry out his predetermined mission. This trip would allow him to follow his route on the ground noting likely choke points, possible ambush sites, potential hides and harbour areas and crossing points of the various water obstacles. This would also allow him to plot targets for possible fire missions. The Sergeant had been very helpful, furnishing him with local knowledge as they travelled along. As they moved, he automatically scanned the terrain ahead although it was unnecessary as this part of the route would have been pacified by the time his Battalion got here. As a third line Motor Rifle Battalion, it only consisted of three companies of BTR 70's which were lightly armed and armoured. Each could carry a crew of 11 but were fully amphibious and the ground pressure of the tyres could be controlled by the driver automatically. This meant that they were able to travel across country and weren't reliant on bridges. His mission was to bypass any potential enemy and seize The RAF base at Gutersloh. Other NATO airfields further west would be the subject of aerial attack to destroy them and deny their use but Gutersloh would be required for Soviet air operations west of The Rhine. Having said that, if it became a political or tactical imperative, it may become the target of a chemical attack. It was reportedly defended by elements of The RAF Regiment with CVR (T)'s but he could call on a flight of FROGFOOT ground attack aircraft for support. The area around here was very attractive and looked more like The Tyrol or Hungary. The Sergeant pointed out the wooden framed Biedermeier houses whose style dated back to the

middle ages and the huge barns whose doors were hand painted with family trees going back generations. He had previously been stationed on the North German Coast, his mission there to capture Kiel and Hamburg before turning north to annexe Denmark. Being Latvian he found the architecture there to be more like his homeland. Not so long ago in history the various countries around The Baltic had belonged to The Hanseatic League, an earlier version of The EU. His own ancestors had in fact been German.

He noticed the little German scout helicopter and thought how smart and modern it looked. Russian aircraft were for the most part, reverse engineered versions of western designs but weren't finished to the same standard. Up close, they looked rough, with protruding rivet heads and mechanical controls and instrumentation. Almost everything in The Soviet arsenal was a copy of a Western design, even the AK47's.They were so basic that they could be turned out in backstreet workshops all over The Third World. They were so badly engineered that you could abuse them, fail to clean them and even swap the parts from other weapons. Because they were basic, they were ideal for uneducated ethnic groups all over the world. That thought made his mind turn to the unit he now commanded. They were typical of the Soviet military. Recruited from all over The Soviet Union, they only spoke very rudimentary Russian taught during basic training. His infantrymen were proficient in their individual weapons and knew basic infantry tactics but that was all. If they could read and write they might be trained to use radios and if they had some sort of mechanical knowledge, usually from belonging to a state controlled motorcycle club, then they would be trained as drivers. The whole army operated to a given set of instructions and tactics which were set in stone. The use of personal initiative was strongly frowned upon in Communist indoctrination, at any level. The NATO armies had realised this early on and it was their practice to target formation commanders, usually vehicles displaying antennae or, in the early days, flags.

He was envious of the East German Army which always seemed to be superior to the others of The Warsaw Pact.

A few weeks ago in the Officers Mess at Magdeburg he had heard two East German officers comment that The Germans spoke better Russian than The Russians. It showed a contempt for their overlords but was true.

It had just turned midnight and Pete had started his second stag. He was in position to guard the track, which each of his crew took in order, two hours on and four hours off. He could easily have taken a position in the O.P. but he liked the solitude and quiet. When the night sky was clear and there was no light pollution he would watch satellites passing over, their trajectories and speed constant, unlike comets and shooting stars which disappeared in an instant. His instincts and senses were also at a heightened state and he was able to distinguish the sounds of different nocturnal animals going about their business. It was amazing what you could see once your eyes had become accustomed to the dark. On occasion, you would even pick up the movement of creatures on the night scopes but he preferred to use his ears

The guys had seemed to have adapted well to the new routine although he had been forced to give a few of the newer ones some advice earlier in the day. One had taken to reading a book, "Wheels of Terror", Sven Hassel and Leo Kessler being required reading across The British Army. Another he had seen rummaging through a ration box for the tin of boiled sweets. For some reason, nobody liked the green ones and he was picking out the others for himself. In both cases he advised them to get some sleep as a priority then wash and eat before resuming their duties. One of the pet sayings of The Squadron Leader was, "sleep is like money in the bank". Very true he thought to himself. Everyone was remembering the lessons of the last years' training, keeping movement and activities in the hide to a minimum. Washing and cleaning kits were kept in the bags which their "crew guard" helmets were stored, and easily at hand, as were their sleeping bags. Meals were prepared as a crew and hot water for washing and shaving. He noticed that they were sleeping with their "Gats" actually inside their sleeping bags with them. This had been ingrained into their consciences with the usual horror stories about SAS sneaking into locations at night and lifting items. If you lost your personal weapon it was a courts martial offence for which you could be imprisoned. At night they would fasten one end of the weapon strap to their wrist. This prevented them from losing them which was easily done.

The possibility of sentries being snatched by The SAS was also stressed as an incentive not to fall asleep. Although they did sometimes steal kit, their usual practice was to spray slogans like "22 SAS" on the vehicles. The fact that they had been able to do it undetected, came as a bit of a shock to the system and had the desired effect. He remembered a previous generation of "old soldiers", in an attempt to impress the new kids, bullshitting about how in Malaya and Borneo, The Gurkhas would sneak up on sentries and tie their bootlaces together. When he had been relieved by Smudger, he made his customary tour of the location, making sure that the guys were putting kit away and that there was no evidence of any unwanted visitors during the night. He also checked the trip flares and the state of the batteries in the O.P. vehicle. It wasn't necessary for him to find his sleeping bag, preferring to wear his German Army issue parka in hide locations. Fleece lined and waterproof, it had a scooped back to protect the kidneys from the cold which also acted as a padded cushion. The cushion could be released and after donning a couple of carrier bags over his boots and drawing them inside, the whole thing could be fastened up to form a sleeping bag. Providing decent kit to its troops wasn't an important consideration of The Army who were inclined to purchase their own. A mail order company on The Old Mile Road in London called Silverman's, who advertised in

"Soldier" magazine was the main provider of waterproofs and cold weather gear. Everyone sported the fleeced "Norgie" shirts and Gore-Tex breathable waterproofs. Three quarter length Barbour jackets were popular as well and the new fashion was a zip which could be laced into your boots. The old DMS boots of First World War vintage has finally given way to a high leg version which was more waterproof and practical but was a nuisance to put on in the dark.

On deployments the Army looked like a bunch of mercenaries or tramps. In comparison The Americans always looked professional, clean and well groomed. Pete could remember an occasion when his regiment had moved into a training camp at Rheinsehlen at the end of an exercise. An American unit was leaving and had thrown all their dirty and used gear in a pile for burning. The Brits had been all over it. These type of incidents were common and had induced The Americans to refer to The British Army as "The borrowers". In response, they were known as "All the gear, no idea".

During the night, undetected by the O.P. a reconnaissance team of The Bundeswehr had monitored the hide activity from the tree line across the valley. Using thermal imagers they had not been able to detect the vehicles but two bright yellow orbs bobbing about announced the presence of its occupants. The vehicles were no doubt concealed in the hollow to the rear. This was their back yard and the position was well known to all the teams within the Brigade. The Feldwebel who was the team leader wondered if they had found the "stash". Drink was forbidden on exercises and it was known for teams to visit the location beforehand and bury crates of beer and spirits. These would be left in place and topped up by other teams as a gesture of good will. They used the laser designator to illuminate the O.P. getting an accurate bearing and distance to the target before moving back 50 meters and reappearing 200 meters along the tree line. They repeated the procedure again, relaying the target reference point to the gun line 10 kilometres behind them. The 155mm battery of the Brigade Artillery Group would only assign one gun to the target. First the O.P. and then the hide would be hit with one round each of an airburst fragmentation shell. The laser was accurate to 10 meters but this was irrelevant as the killing zone of the shell was 150 meters.

It was a sobering thought to the Feldwebel that other teams had made the same prediction for his survival when he had previously occupied this position.

At 08:00 Pete had ended his stag and changed his routine. Instead of going to sleep he mounted the wagon for the expected "stand to" from 08:15 until 09:15. Smudger was on guard down the track but he noticed that Nick had stowed all the gear on the wagon and was ready in the turret. A little while later the distinctive sound of a Land Rover could be heard dragging itself through the wheel ruts of the approach track. The enemy didn't use Land Rovers so it was nothing to worry about. It was a sure sign that something was about to happen though.

Down the track, Smudger appeared out of the shadows and challenged the driver, even though he recognised him. "Echo Golf" he offered, and the driver, Porky as he was known replied "Golf Sierra".

"Well done lad" came from the character in the passenger side.

Bloody hell, it's the regular Sar'nt Major, Ron Andrews he thought.

"Pull in over there "he indicated, "The hide's about 100 meters further on, keep to the track, we've laid flares". Parking inside the trees the two made their way up to the hide, Smudger noticed that they had picked up thunderflashes and smoke grenades from the back of the wagon. Giving them a couple of minute's head start, he began to move back to the hide as Pete had told him. As he approached the hide Ron started appraising what he saw. The crews were mounted and the kit all stored, only the cam nets and bivvies were deployed. He was also aware of a sentry up wind of the hide in full NBC kit. After a nod of recognition to The Troop Sergeant George Stafford, he followed the command wire to the O.P. itself, Porky remained behind. George announced to the crews, "Fucking switch on now, something's going to happen".

CHAPTER FOUR

WITHDRAWAL IN CONTACT

For the duration of the exercise, all of the PSI's across the regiment had been tasked with the role of umpire. Ron had been assigned to 1st Troop and to display his status he wore a white armband. His Land Rover was also decorated with white mine tape. He was in direct contact with his opposite number attached to the Bundeswehr unit across the valley. They had some idea of what was going to happen, their main purpose though was to decide on the results of any action which was simulated. In the first phase they had agreed that an artillery strike on The British O.P. line would initiate a withdrawal allowing The Germans to advance.

Approaching the O.P. Ron noticed that the far tree line was still clear of the enemy and engaged the team in conversation for a while. He casually asked about emergency R.V's and the S.O.P. should the location be attacked, noticing that this troop seemed to have everything covered. The site was immaculate and should they have to "crash out" they were prepared for it. Out of the corner of his eye he could see vehicles appearing where the main road left the tree line. He was ready to initiate the artillery strike but held off, giving the team time to get off a contact report.

It was the Corporal who saw them first, "CONTACT" he announced before turning in the direction of the hide and screaming "STAND TO"!! His alarm was answered within seconds by the sound of engines starting up.

The P.S.I. nodded with satisfaction as the contact report was sent out, the Troop Leader had already formatted the coded message in anticipation of the event.

"Hello 0, this is Charlie 10, 3 Kilo, sierra/foxtrot/hotel (Break radio silence) contact as at 09:00 hours, Grid 402 912, 1 Luchs, 2 Fuchs moving south on the candy stripe, observing over".

"Hello Charlie 10 this is 0, roger, out to you. Hello all callsigns this is 0, 3 Lima, papa/golf/sierra (lift radio silence) out".

Charlie jumped unexpectedly as the thunderflash exploded behind him "That was a 155, your dead" announced The Sergeant Major gleefully before turning and moving towards the hide.

Back at the hide, as discussed earlier, Porky began dropping thunderflashes everywhere, noticing that the sentries were already running back to the hide. Within seconds three of the Foxes were tearing down the track, the cam nets of the garages billowing outwards. The last vehicle was dragging his behind him but it snagged on something and dropped to the ground. As the remaining fox burst into life, Ron shouted at the driver "Don't bother mate, your dead".

Turning to face Charlie as he ran up, he quickly declared "Your crew is out of it, you will remain here until the end of this phase is announced and then make your way back to SHQ". Porky was already moving and Ron ran after him his adrenaline flowing. This is what he lived for he thought, bugger the grandkids and bugger retirement.

At the R.V. the rest of the troop had deployed for all round defence while they waited for Charlie to catch up. In the meantime, they listened to the contact reports coming in, the Squadron had been hit everywhere by artillery and George waited for a gap in the radio traffic to call in.

"Hello 0 this is Charlie 11, Shellrep as at 09:00 hours, Grid 402 912, 2 rounds of 155, this location compromised, new locstat to follow, out".

As he pulled up Ron told him, "They were caught in the open, their all dead, push on mate".

Tapping the top of his helmet with the flat of his hand George indicated to the two other commanders to join him.

"They're fucked, we will move along this track to the main road to set up an ambush position, make sure your turrets are pointing to the rear".

Back at the hide Charlie felt dejected that he had been killed so quickly and would now miss out on the next part of the exercise, probably the best part. He had spent 2 days sat in a hole in the ground bored shitless, he might as well have joined the Infantry.

"Might as well get some breakfast on" he announced to the others. Then we'll take down the hide and get some kip".

The wood was still full of smoke caused by the pyro and he could hear "Johnny Rotten "and his crew squealing as they scurried around, setting off the trip flares in their panic.

As they broke out onto the road, 1st Troop swung south and carried on over the first rise, passing Support troop who looked to have established a "30 second ambush". Once over it George and Pete pulled onto opposite sides of the road and reversed back to assume a turret down stance while Jack carried on for about 500 meters, finding an over watch position.

With only their heads visible over the rise they watched and waited for whatever would happen next.

Looking back down the hill through his binoculars Pete could see that the traffic had been stopped out on the valley floor. A good indicator that something was about to happen.

At the bottom of the hill a long, high vehicle edged into view, it was a Luchs. The Luchs, meaning Lynx in English, was a fully amphibious 8 wheeled reconnaissance vehicle mounting a 20mmm cannon in a turret and a crew of four. To assist in contact situations it had two drivers, one at either end. It was big for a recce vehicle, probably twice the size of a Fox and super quiet. Its engine seemed to purr when it passed by you. Following behind it were two Fuchs or Foxes, 6 wheeled amphibious APC's which carried an infantry section of ten men, both of them carrying a TOW launcher.

Support Troop allowed them to move up the hill and when they were broadside on, all three were engaged simultaneously with Charlie G's, 84mm anti-tank guns from about 50 meters. These were simulated by the no 2's throwing thunder flashes. They immediately ran back into the trees about 50 meters before turning south, parallel to the road to re-join the three Spartans waiting in a concealed hide. As the German infantry sections dismounted they were engaged by two GPMG's one on either side of the road which were able to fire down both sides of the vehicles. They each expended one belt of 200 rounds before falling back out of site and crossing the road to re-join their troop. The umpires obviously considered the ambush to be effective as all three vehicles were motioned off the road along with the two infantry sections. In the distance two specs appeared in the sky each had huge turbofan engines on the side of the fuselage and positioned so as to be shielded by the wings from ground fire…A10's. Easily recognisable, Pete had seen them perform at firepower demonstrations and knew what they were capable of. The whole aircraft was built around a 20mm Vulcan cannon firing tungsten tipped anti-armour shells. The pilot sat in an armoured bath to protect him from ground fire. It could make Swiss cheese of anything on the battlefield.

The first one cruised straight up the road and Pete ducked instinctively as it passed over, had they overshot? Then he realised that The Spartans had been forced by the terrain to exit the wood, onto the road. He watched as the second one, there was always two, swung out to the side and strafed the Spartans on a line 45 degrees from the road. It was a classic ground attack.

The accompanying umpire obviously thought so too as they were pulled off the road.

At the bottom of the hill a new group of vehicles appeared.

They were unaware of 1st Troop and moved past the first group.

At a nod from George, Pete simultaneously reversed up the rise into a hull down position.

Most crews were happy just to shout "BANG" when simulating an engagement but Pete, like George, insisted in following the correct fire orders. Drills were there for a reason and he could here George screaming at Briggsy, his gunner.

Putting his face to the sight he began…."Shot on, 800 meters, armoured car in open"

"800 on"

"Loaded, fire"

"Firing now…Target".

"Target stop, driver advance".

At the same time he threw out a thunder flash.

Nick pulled the wagon forward, dropping below the crest of the road. Pete noticed that George had chosen to engage a second target and had stayed in position. Ron Andrews, still with his umpires head on jumped onto his wagon and shouted "You're dead", to which George replied "Fuck off, what are you on about man"?

"You're fucking dead, the 3rd wagon engaged you with his TOW".

Not waiting to hear the rest of the heated debate, Pete took off down the road passing Jack and then the Spartans.

As he passed them he noticed that they had unwillingly accepted their fate. Most were stood about with a fag in their mouths and a brew in their hands while others were pissing up the side of the wagons.

Once he had gone firm, Jack leap frogged him in turn and they both withdrew down the other side of the ridge before finding another fire position.

After a while it became obvious that things had come to a halt. The civilian traffic had been released and began to stream past, the occupants scowling at them.

"Fucking box heads" Nick retorted, "Don't they realise they're an occupied country"?   After 40 years the population of areas like this probably had a right to be pissed thought

Pete, but in peace time nobody wanted The Army. Kipling had it right though he thought…..

"and it's Tommy this and Tommy that and Tommy how's your soul, but it's thin red line of heroes when the drums begin to roll".

"Hello all stations this is 0, this phase is over, move to 4 Alpha, Grid, Victor, Tango, Romeo, Mike, Romeo, Romeo Out".

Nick shouted across to Jack, "I suggest we move to the obvious feature at the crossroads in Eschershausen". Jack had nodded his approval and they had made their way to the Schnelle, as did a good part of the squadron.

The new location given for SHQ was about 6 miles back down the valley from the original. It turned out to be a forest just east of the village of Lobach. The squadron was greatly reduced in size, 1st, 3rd and 5th Troops had each lost 2 wagons, 4th was still intact but 2nd and Boot Troop had been completely destroyed. SHQ now consisted of 1 Sultan and The Ferret.

Following a de-brief by The Squadron Leader and a description of the actual facts from various sources, the fate of The Squadron was revealed.

1st, 2nd and 3rd which had formed the actual O.P. line had all received similar attention from German Artillery. Whereas 1st had lost 1 wagon, 3rd had lost 2 and had moved to the opposite side of the ridge and supported 4th in defending the open flank to the south east.

On reaching 2nd Troops location, the umpire had been amazed at the state of the hide. The sentry had greeted him with a "thumbs up", not bothering to challenge him. The hide itself was in chaos, kit everywhere, some guys cooking, others washing, some even still in their pits. They should have been "stood to". At the O.P. itself, which was mounted, the crew were chatting amongst themselves and totally oblivious to the two vehicles in the opposite tree line flashing their headlights at them to signify that they were being engaged.

The umpire had detonated his thunder flash screaming at the crew "You are all fucking dead".

On returning to the hide, throwing more thunder flashes on the way and even a yellow smoke to signify gas, the rest of the troop had still not responded, some of them looking around in confusion. The troop Leader was still "fannying about" with his shaving kit. Striding up to The Troop Sergeant he repeated, "YOU ARE ALL FUCKING DEAD YOU SLACK BASTARD", the last remark was aimed directly at him.

He informed his opposite number on the other side of the valley that the location had been totally destroyed. When The Squadron Leader was later informed he was not impressed.

4th Troop had been observing from the end of a ridge on the southern side of the main valley which ran south easterly from Eschershausen. They had set up a fire mission on the crossroads in the village of Muhlenbeck. They had remained undetected throughout and were never engaged.

Unfortunately, the units that approached Muhlenbeck didn't use the crossroads. Consisting of tracked vehicles they passed the village, choosing to go off road and 4th Troop were unable to bring them under artillery fire. They were forced to fall back in order not to be outflanked.

5th Troop who were acting as reserve and at SHQ's location were sent off to investigate reports of a Heli borne landing at Oelkassen, 1 mile north. Between the two locations was the spur of a forest which shielded it from view. With no cross country capability and the intervening fields bordered by ditches, the Troop had been forced to use a circuitous route to get there.

They exited the forest in time to see four Sea Stallion helicopters disappearing over the horizon. In the field in front of them stood 2 Sections of what one trooper described as looking like giant Toads. They were in fact Weasels, something new to most of the Squadron. Even smaller than the Fox they had a 3 man crew and could be armed with either a 20mm cannon or a Milan anti-tank weapon. Used by German Airborne Units they were air portable and very fast, being powered by Audi 100 engines

A battle developed which resulted in the destruction of 5 of the Weasels for the loss of 2 Foxes. The remaining 3 bypassed 5th Troop and due to their size were able to move through the forest. Raising the alarm, 5th Troop gave chase but had to stick to the road. From the edge of the forest the Weasels engaged SHQ at a range of about 600 meters.

Totally out gunned and out ranged, SHQ lost one of the Sultans, the Samaritan, the Samson and 2 Spartans which were providing force protection.

Only the second Sultan and Ferret escaped. Appearing on their flank, the 2 surviving foxes destroyed the last of the Weasels.

Throughout the rest of the day the fragmented Squadron slowly came together in the forest at Lobach and licked its wounds.

CHAPTER FIVE

ADVANCE TO CONTACT

As contact had been lost with the opposing force, The Squadron Leader needed to know just how far they had advanced.

He was also concerned about the forest which spread to the north of his present location and intended to put out a number of foot patrols who would exploit to its far side. From there they would also be able to observe across the bowl of farmland which spread for about 3 km to the next wooded ridgeline. He informed his Support Troop Leader of his intentions and it was agreed that 3 fighting patrols of 6 men each would infiltrate it that night and establish O.P's on its northern edge. The road from The River Weser split to run either side of the forest, the left hand one running back up towards Eschershausen, this was the route which they had withdrawn down. The right hand one led to the town of Stadtoldendorf. Both of these, he believed had been occupied. Joining them was a shallow wooded ridge, it was a formidable defensive position. Dependant on the information acquired by these patrols, he would exploit up both valleys tomorrow morning.

The Support Troop Commander was Captain Johnathon Walton, known as "John Boy" because of the character in the TV show, "The Waltons".

He had taken up a short service commission after leaving University, The Army having subsidised his education. Much to the pleasure of his Father, he had followed him into The Devon and Dorsets, completing one tour in Ulster before being posted to The Light Infantry Depot at Winchester. Having graduated as a chemist, on leaving The Regular Army, he had secured a position with a pharmaceutical company, but found to his surprise that there was an aspect of the military which he missed. This had prompted him to join The Territorial Army Volunteer Reserves.

A subconscious decision was made to allow his 3 junior vehicle commanders to lead the patrols. Untethered to their Troop Sergeant and Officer, the independence would be good for them. He had no doubt that they were all more than capable. He made them aware of the aims of the action and the time frame which they would have to work to. Everything else was left to them. Putting their heads together during what The Army called "a Chinese parliament", they later presented their plan to him which he accepted.

As one of the more junior NCO's in Boot Troop, Wayne Travis had been astounded when he was given command of a Spartan for this exercise. The prospect of leading a section on a scheme which he had to plan himself was something else altogether.

He had no doubt that he could do it and that the guys he chose would follow him, his only concern was that he would fail the test and let The Boss down. Having been born in Australia, his parents had decided to return to "The Old Country" when he was still a kid. Retaining his Australian accent, the boys called him "Digger". He was a farm labourer by trade and his size and disposition showed that. Fitter than anybody else in The Troop, weapons that the others struggled to carry looked like toys in his hands.

As well as the 4 guys in his own section he decided to take one other from another wagon which was supposed to remain behind. As a former member of The Recce platoon in a Regular Battalion, Digger knew that the guy had the skills and experience for this job. Taking the team to one side he explained that the job would involve a night patrol through the forest to establish an O.P. Which they would maintain until first light before returning to this location. They might be compromised and so as well as the equipment for the O.P. they would have to be capable of defending themselves. They would be out and back within 9 hours so personal equipment would be kept to a minimum with belt order only.

They would each carry an SLR with 60 rounds apiece and one smoke grenade or thunder flash, their first field dressing, a full water bottle, sufficient cold rations, (there would be no cooking), if they wished to take cold weather gear they would have to wear it, no waterproofs or headgear and they would of course be blacked up. Each man would also carry a rolled up piece of cam net measuring 6'x6'.

He then gave them their specific roles, indicating to them as he went.

Lead scout and navigator was obvious.

One guy would carry the backpack and spare battery. He himself would have the map, compass, torch and spare batteries, as well as the frequencies and codes. Together they would form the actual O.P. team.

One would be the team medic with a medical pack and sleeping bag in case of emergencies.

The other two would be there simply as backup and to provide extra firepower if needed.

Once they had sorted out their individual equipment, they practiced the drills and hand signals which would be used.

HALT, GO TO GROUND, DEPLOY LEFT OR RIGHT, RALLY ON ME, ALLROUND DEFENCE, EMERGENCY RV and ENEMY CLOSE.

They also practiced contact drills and casualty retrieval as well as the body search of enemy casualties.

When he was happy he advised them to get some hot food, rehydrate and sleep.

An hour before the appointed time he woke them and checked that they had no loose kit, were blacked up and knew the passwords bearing in mind that they would have changed on return. On the way out of the Squadron hide he counted them off and confirmed with the sentry how many there would be on return, passwords and the bearing they would approach from.

Hoping that he had covered everything, he followed the team out of the hide, unaware that his troop Leader was watching him from the shadows.

The wood was darker than he expected, just inside it they stopped for 10 minutes to improve their night vision. This had been covered in the briefing. As they moved off in single file, Whiskey, the lead scout looked at the compass taped to the butt of his SLR. He had intended to use this and count his paces to move through the forest but it was unnecessary. The trees had been planted in neat rows running in the direction that they were traveling with a set distance between them to help with harvesting.

It was easier just to count the trees. Using the fire breaks which ran across their route at right angles to confirm his theory, he discovered that he was spot on. At each firebreak, they crossed singly covering each other. At the last one before the edge of the forest, he indicated to Digger that this was the emergency R.V. This was signalled back down the line via the radio op, medic and finally the two backup guys. About 200 meters before the tree line Whiskey stopped to check his navigation and almost immediately was aware of noise and movement ahead.

Using hand signals he informed Digger who in turn motioned the team to come up in line abreast and take position behind trees. He didn't really want them to lie down in case they had to withdraw, and so indicated that they should take a kneeling position.

At about 20 meters he initiated the firefight and noticed that the enemy group fell back in two teams of two, using short bounds to cover each other, one team moving and the other providing covering fire. This was exactly what they had practised earlier that afternoon and it told him that these guys were well trained. It was over in thirty seconds and after five minutes they advanced slowly in line abreast. When they could see the treeline and the open fields beyond, Digger indicated that the team should deploy for all round defence and with his radio man found a location behind one of the few fallen trees further on.

They covered themselves with the nets and he scoured the moonlit landscape before him, picking up the hedgerow which the enemy must have used to approach the forest. They were well and truly alone. The rest of the team made shallow shell scrapes and covered themselves with the nets, forming a circle with their boots touching. This meant that two could sleep at a time while the other two covered opposite arcs. It would only take a touch of the boot to alert everyone.

Digger had lost his night vision during the firefight and it was still returning and so he used his hearing instead. The idea was that you should keep one eye closed to prevent this but the reality was entirely different. He could easily hear the two other patrols either side of him moving up, "noisy bastards" he thought to himself. They settled into their routine and he began making out a fire plan as the moon moved in and out of the clouds.

Back at their Audi 4WD, the Gefreiter who had led the patrol reflected on the skirmish. If he had been stationary whilst the enemy had been moving their roles would have been reversed with him initiating the firefight. He would more likely to have laid mines as they withdrew but they had lost the initiative. Their fire discipline had been good, the distinctive sound of the SLR's marking them as British. But he had achieved his mission goals.

At the agreed time, they broke camp and retraced their steps. As they passed the site of the ambush Digger noticed that there was no sign of the enemy's bullet cases. Did they have spent cartridge collectors on their weapons or had they been professional enough to actually pick them up? Their own cases were easy to see.

As they approached the squadron hide he signalled the team to go to ground as he made himself known to the sentry. Exchanging the password challenge and response he then motioned the team forward, counting them off to make sure nobody had joined their group.

Back at the wagons they lined up and at his command cleared their weapons before presenting them to him for inspection. "Clean yer weapons and then try to get some kip" he told them before making his way to the CV.

Both The Boss and the Squadron Leader seemed happy with his report, but not as happy as he was having completed the task.

He also felt completely knackered and couldn't wait to get into his pit, noticing that the others were already snoring away.

At the O GROUP the next day the Squadron Leader was very demonstrative. He had attended a conference at Brigade HQ earlier that morning to find out why **HIS** Squadron was being left out of the current exercise plan. It turned out that the new Brigade Commander had previously commanded an Infantry Battalion and had no concept of the ability of a Light Reconnaissance Regiment. That was why the whole Regiment had been tasked with establishing an O.P. line for two days.

Luckily, The Deputy Brigade Commander was a former C.O. of The Regiment and was able to open his eyes as to what he could do with 100 odd light armoured vehicles with large fuel tanks who could act independently for anything up to a week.

They had been given a new task.

"Gentlemen, it is my intention to make a demonstration North East towards the Negenborn/Stadtoldendorf feature and to use speculative fire to establish the enemy's positions. Once exposed, a WARRIOR combat team will close with them and destroy them". He indicated his instructions on the laminated wall map as he talked. The various villages and junctions were indicated with 2 figure code numbers.

"3rd Troop will move up the L583 (SPARROW) to the railway bridge designated Nick 49 securing these three junctions en-route".

"Simultaneously, 2nd Troop will move up the B64 (ROBIN) in the direction of Negenborn, with 4th Troop supporting from the direction of Nick 61".

"5th Troop will leave SPARROW at Nick 31 to approach the village of Deensen, before exploiting north on FINCH".

"1st Troop will proceed to Braak, via Nick 99 and 73 in order to move along "SWALLOW".

"This will allow The Squadron to move towards the objective in line abreast along four parallel routes".

"Once the enemy has been identified, the combat team will close with them".

After being informed of the timings, supporting units and other information relevant to the task, Charlie looked at the trace and recognised that he would be open to attack from his right. For most of the length of route SWALLOW, he would be overlooked by the wooded hills of The Holzbergwiesen.

He returned to The Troop to begin the briefing, thankful that 1st would be the last to move. Being the last troop to leave they were able to cruise at a steady speed, Charlie deciding that they would be in two separate groups, Pete Wood leading with him in support and then Sharpie with George bringing up the rear. To Charlie's mind, being in the centre, he could maintain control both forward and back but as far as George was concerned it placed him at risk and their places should have been reversed.

As they pulled out onto the road the inevitable Ron Andrews followed, raising the quip from Briggsy, "That guy's like dogshit....everywhere".

When they turned off SPARROW at Nick 99, the troop closed up and off to their 2 o'clock they could see 5th Troop making their flanking move on the village of Deensen. They were supposed to have co-ordinated it with 1st. Of more concern to George was that the junction was also the location of a railway crossing, an obvious target for pre designated artillery.

Each troop had been allocated a Spartan and as they approached the village, Digger pushed on to dismount his section. It made its way to the junction in the centre of the village with the Spartan providing support. Expecting to meet 5th Troop at the junction, they were met instead with the sounds of thunder flashes going off and an armoured vehicle reversing towards them. 200 meters down the road, a Jaguar could be seen with its back to them.

Two of the section immediately ran back to the Spartan and collected the Charlie G, their only means of stopping it and they knelt in the middle of the road to engage it.

"Load"

"Load" came the reply.

"Loaded"

"Loaded, standby"

"Standby"

"Firing, now".

The other two had already opened up with their SLR's and having blocked the junction with the Spartan, Digger also engaged it with his turret mounted GPMG.

Ron Andrews appeared as if by magic and throwing a thunder flash and smoke grenade announced that The Jaguar was dead.

The Jaguar was a reincarnation of the 2nd World War Jagerpanzer IV but fitted with a TOW anti-tank missile system. The opposing German commander had obviously deployed a number forward of his main defence line as a screen.

With the Jaguar pulled off the road, 5th Troop were able to pass.

Pete noticed that two of the Foxes were missing and their umpire confirmed that they had been claimed by the Jaguar. With the residents of the village looking on in disbelief, 5th pressed on to begin their move up route FINCH while 1st made towards the village of Braak.

As they moved, Pete couldn't help but think that the scenario and terrain was very similar to that of an engagement involving The Regiment in Normandy 40 years before, known as St Nicholas Farm. Clear of the village on the left hand side of the road was a farm complex, beyond it open countryside and in the distance at 10 o'clock was a tree line. They had claimed 13 MKIV's and 4 Tigers amongst their kills that day. It was ironic he thought, that the opposing forces today were again German.

The plan had been to enter the village along a road from the south, (SWALLOW) but Charlie decided that they would leave the road and deploy in line abreast to approach it from the South West. The open fields and lack of boundary ditches would allow this for a change. They stopped about 500 meters short and at his command opened up with their co-axial machine guns flashing their headlights to signify the main armament being used as well. Hoping to provoke a response, Charlie could see movement in between the houses.

Ron was ringing his hand with excitement as he heard the young "Rupert" call in a fire mission.

"Hello Golf Two Two this is Romeo One Zero, fire mission over".

"Golf Two Two, fire mission over".

"Romeo One Zero, fire mission, Grid 880 140, Direction 50 degrees magnetic, 500 meters, Infantry in village, neutralize now for two minutes, over".

"Golf Two Two, fire mission, Grid 880 140, Direction 50 degrees magnetic, 500 meters, infantry in village, neutralize now for two minutes….one gun adjusting, over".

"One gun adjusting, out".

"Splash one five over".

"Splash one five out".

Fifteen seconds later the supposed ranging round landed and Charlie confirmed "Target, over".

"Target, out". Followed a few minute later by "Rounds complete, over".

"Rounds complete, target neutralized, end of fire mission, over".

"Target neutralized, end of fire mission, out".

Totally immersed in the task, Charlie was unaware of the arrival of a company of Warriors who turned off the road and deployed either side of them.

"Hello all stations Romeo One Zero, this is Romeo One Zero, retire 300 meters out".

As the Troop moved, the line of 12 Warriors advanced until about 100 meters from the edge of the village, deployed their sections and promptly reversed 300 meters to provide supporting fire. According to the drill, this would take them out of affective RPG range.

They watched and listened as the infantry cleared the village, followed by the Warriors who broke in on three farm tracks, one of them crashing through a wooden gate.

"Bloody hooligans" Ron commented to his driver Porky who wasn't convinced by his sincerity.

Bypassing the village, Charlie led The Troop along route SWALLOW to a bend in the road where they deployed in a box formation for all round defence. Stadtoldendorf was 500 meters ahead.

Directly from their right came the sound of a thunder flash, announcing the arrival of a Milan round from a hedgerow.

The Troop immediately "Brassed up" the hedge and a German wearing the white armband of an umpire emerged to approach Ron Andrews' Land Rover.

"The Milan team are dead but your lead wagon has been destroyed, only the gunner has survived, deal with it".

Motioning the Spartan to move up to him, Charlie shouted at Digger as it drew alongside.

"That wagon has been hit, only the gunner has survived, evacuate him".

Moving up to the Fox, the four guys in the back of the Spartan climbed onto the Fox's back deck and pulled out Smudger but as they transferred him onto the front of the Spartan he accidently grabbed the exhaust, badly scolding himself in the process.

In the back of the Spartan, as it reversed away, they dealt with his now very real injury. Jocko, the section medic had them fill a dixie with cold water which they immersed his hand into. It was Jocko's opinion that he would need more treatment though and George told them to evacuate him to the Samaritan.

As the Spartan sped back across the fields Pete could hear Digger raising The Samaritan on the net.

"Hello Romeo 14 Bravo, this is Echo 22 Delta, NO DUFF, one casualty with severe burns to the hand, send your location over".

The NO DUFF would let everyone know that this wasn't an exercise.

"Hello Echo 22 Delta, this is Romeo 14 Bravo, RV at Grid 860 160, out".

Looking at the map, Pete could see that it was the wood yard back at the junction, Nick 99. It would literally take 5 minutes to get there.

"Can I have his beer?" came from Nick Shields, his driver. You got no sympathy in The Army.

Back at the wood yard, which was now SHQ's location, The Squadron Leader decided that he could write this incident into the exercise plan and sent for both the Squadron medic and the Staff Sergeant who ran his LAD detachment.

On his arrival Smudger was treated by the Squadron medic, his hand being sealed in a special glove which would keep
the wound sterile and prevent it being exposed to air, which would cause it to sting. It had blistered badly and his fingers were fused together. Confirming that he needed further attention, The Squadron Leader told his driver to take him to the BMH at Rinteln.
Staying on "SWALLOW", Charlie deployed the other two wagons onto two tracks which ran parallel to it, facing towards any threat from the direction of Stadtoldendorf. Listening to the net, it sounded as if the rest of The Squadron had also encountered Jaguars with varying success.

Half an hour later the LAD and Samaritan arrived and simulated the recovery of the Fox and its crew. In reality it would not have been recovered. Being made of aluminium armour, the kinetic energy of any armour defeating round hitting it would cause it to burn and deform. Pete remembered on a D+M course at Bovvy, talking to a Jordanian who had experience of being in a Scorpion which was hit. The body had warped so much that some of the hatches couldn't be opened. With extreme heat they could even weld shut, trapping the crew. No wonder then that they couldn't sell it to foreign armies. Good enough for the British Army though. With the assistance of the fitters, the Samaritan crew recovered the two bodies, going through the process of removing private items and "tagging+bagging" the remains.

It was a sobering experience to all involved and was taken seriously. The fox was recovered by the LAD and returned to the wood yard with Pete and Nick traveling in the back of the Samaritan.

According to the rules they were out of it until the end of this phase and they made the most of a good wash and shave followed by some scran and more than a few "Herdy Ferdies"

At Rinteln things were not going well for Smudger. He was going to need extensive surgery and skin grafts back in The UK and the doctors were concerned about some of his behaviour. He was analysed and they determined that he had advanced OCD which in turn revealed that he was mildly autistic. His time in the military was coming to an end and he was about to lose the only people in his life who seemed to both like and accept him.

With the end of this phase, The Squadron returned to the forest at Lobach, performing a "Tailboard Replen" at a quarry en-route. The "Tailboard Replen" involved The Squadron, in Troop packets, meeting up with the 4 Tonners of Admin Troop in a concealed location, usually on a forested track. Admin Troop consisted of three 4 Tonners and a Land Rover. The 4 Tonners were designated as P.O.L. (petrol, oil and lubricants), Ammo and G10 (Rations water and clothing) respectfully.

Vehicles would pull up to them, and in the case of G10 would receive rations including ARMY baked bread and new Jerries of water. Army bread had the day it was baked printed on the wrapper, if it was a Monday you could bet that the wrapper said Tuesday.

Ammo being distributed on an exercise was unheard of, even pyro.

With the P.O.L. wagon, the driver would shout up to the turret crew what he required, with the 20 litre Jerries being stored on the turret or rear storage bin. The vehicle commander would have to give his name and last 4 digits of his Army number and the vehicle reg. They were then guided to a separate location where the crew refuelled and dropped the empty cans off. As a rule the driver and gunner would refuel while the commander stood guard from the turret. With the demise of Smudger, Pete and Nick had to

sort it themselves. If time allowed a crewmember would return to the G10 wagon to negotiate the sale of cigarettes, fresh meat, eggs and beer.

CHAPTER SIX

WITHDRAWAL AND RESERVE DEMO

Returning from the O GROUP later that evening, Charlie was approached by the whole TROOP. "Any news on Smudger Boss?" Nick asked.

"He's being returned to the UK for surgery, can you police up his kit and secure his SMG please Corporal Wood"?

"Boss" he replied.

"Vehicle commanders on me if you please" he carried on. As the rest of The Troop retired he spread out his map on the back deck of a wagon, Pete noticing the new traces on it.

"The Division is withdrawing to the other side of The Weser, each of the three Brigades by a separate route and river crossing". He demonstrated on the map. A Squadron will be controlling the move for 49 Brigade and crossing the river at this point here". He pointed to the area of the village of Herstelle. "The actual bridge has been destroyed for exercise reality, a temporary one being provided by an M2 Squadron of The Royal Engineers".

(The M2 was an amphibious vehicle which could be used on its own as a ferry or joined with others to form a bridge).

"The route is designated FISH and the three harbour areas
TROUT, CARP and PERCH. The bridge itself will be SALMON"

They followed his finger across the map making notes and copying the markings as he indicated them.

"TROUT, the concentration area, will be at Altenhagen and controlled by 3rd Troop. CARP, the harbour area, this side of the river at this point on the B241, controlled by 4th Troop and PERCH, the release point, in the area north of Hasselhof by 5th".

"ZERO will control the move and be situated at the bridge itself with ZERO BRAVO at TROUT and ZERO Charlie at PERCH, no packet will move unless directed by him".

"The LAD will also operate from TROUT and provide recovery along the whole route. Boot Troop is to deploy at the crossroads at Silberborn to prevent any enemy attempt to cut the road".

"We will be escorting the packets between TROUT and CARP where we will hand over to 2nd Troop. Any questions? No? Good. The route must be established by 21:00 tonight".

"It might be an idea for us to recce our section of the route beforehand, so that we can identify any potential problems" stated George.

"I've been here before Sir, the junction at Neuhaus switches back on itself and will be a choke point, and we may have to find a detour" Pete piped up.

Once again, Corporal Wood with his foresight thought Charlie.

"I managed to attain something from the Squadron Leader's Land Rover," He said, holding up a bottle of JAGERMEISTER. "See that the guys all get a swig, it's going to be a long night. Ready to move at 18:00 hours".

As they split up, Charlie made a conscious effort to have a wash and brush his teeth, he felt decidedly grubby and had a mouth "like Ghandi's flip flop".

The concentration area was a field accessed by driving through a small hamlet off to the side of the main road and Pete once again felt sorry for the locals. It was a pretty little place and had the usual aura of German efficiency and smartness. He knew what was about to happen throughout this day and the next, the village would look dirty and dusty after the passing of hundreds of vehicles, the road destroyed and torn up. An Army "Damage control team" would show up afterwards to make repairs and clean up the mud. They would even offer financial compensation to the residents but The Army's presence would still be resented.

The troop drove the route as discussed, confirming Pete's description of the junction at Neuhaus and a diversion was plotted along the edge of a nearby forest which would bypass it.

Parts of the route were narrow with no passing places but it would be a one-way system with all civilian traffic being diverted by the local Police Force and elements of 116 PROVOST COMPANY RMP. Being a TA Infantry Brigade, they possessed no heavy artillery or main battle tanks, with most of their vehicles being wheeled.

Obvious ambush points and water obstacles were also noted. Although they travelled the route as a Troop, each commander made his own observations and a "Chinese parliament" was convened afterwards to discuss their findings and come up with resolutions.

The routine and drills of harbour areas and controlled moves were the "bread and butter" of armoured car units, especially in rear areas. The only real resistance could come from Heli borne and Special Forces units or ground attack aircraft.

As the various units reached the concentration area they were divided up into packets with the first and last vehicles being marked with coloured grease on one of their headlights. Blue on the first and green on the last. This was signified by flags during daylight. The number of vehicles and packet numbers were recorded, this information being passed on ahead to the various traffic control points.

It was 1ˢᵗ Troop's job to shepherd them from the concentration area to the next harbour area where control was passed to 2ⁿᵈ Troop. The troop worked in pairs, moving at a controlled speed the manoeuvres went on throughout the night and well into the second day. It seemed to become an endless carousel with only a few mechanical

problems to break the routine. Although it was impressive, it was nothing compared to Exercise Lionheart in 1984. Pete could remember being on a bridge guard where the packets consisted of 100 plus wagons each, were nose to tail andhad taken 24 hours to pass his location. That had reportedly been the biggest mobilization of The British Army since Normandy in '44.

The move continued into the afternoon when events changed radically. Support Troop reported that they were in contact and were basically pushed aside by a force of Leopard 1's and Marders. This was a reconnaissance in force by the opposing forces. Having broken through the covering screen they had at last realised what was happening and attempted to trap the remnants of The Brigade east of the river.

With the last of the packets passed on to 2nd Troop, 1st took up a defensive position at the junction in Neuhaus facing the road from Silberborn. Within minutes they witnessed ZERO BRAVO and the LAD passing by at speed.

Although FOX had the ability to use armour defeating ammunition, because of the terrain, they decided to deploy one wagon each on side roads to engage The Leopards from the flanks. On the opposite side of the junction the other two took up positions to enfilade the junction and cover their withdrawal. As the first Leopard passed it was engaged by George and Jack from both sides and Ron Andrews appeared, as if by magic, to dispense his smoke and thunder flashes announcing that it was dead. As the two FOXES withdrew across the junction Pete was amazed to see that two other Leopards had bypassed them and were traveling down a parallel road. He hadn't even heard them and noticed that if they had been Chieftains he'd have heard them miles away, never mind having seen the great plumes of blue smoke that they chucked out. Fortunately that road led into a residential area which was also a cul-de-sac. Once George and Jack had passed, the other two moved, the four of them taking up a new position half a mile back on a bend in the road which would negate the range of The Leopards guns. As they moved, Pete noticed the staff of the village post office out in the street. They looked totally astounded whereas other residents were shouting and gesticulating, waving their arms about and screaming at them, some in English. How they knew that they were British amazed Pete.

Would they give the Leopards the same reception or because they displayed Iron Crosses on their turrets would it be different?

The Germans weren't fooled though and allowed the supporting Marders to deploy their infantry sections into the woods.

Throwing smoke and firing their GPMG's, the troop withdrew down a forest track before boxing around and spilling out onto the road again. Still concealed from the Leopards they dropped back to the village of Shonhagen. The road here formed a hairpin bend and they were able to observe back up the hill from the village. This went on for the next couple of hours, each time forcing the advancing enemy to stop and deploy until Zero announced that the last packet had crossed the river.

Although 1st Troop were the only ones on the enemy's side of the river, the bridge had not yet been prepared for demolition and the rest of The Squadron were deployed again as a screen. Between the bridge and the last village, the land was a collection of flat open fields in the shape of a peninsula. The river was on three sides, with the open neck being the direction which the enemy must approach from. However, the left hand side of the neck had a series of marinas fed by the river and the right a railway embankment. Between them was a gap of about 200 meters through which a road ran.

Charlie, recognising that the approaching force could only come through the gap called for a prepared fire plan to cover it. The road between the gap and the bridge had a number of bends, each one overlooked by some sort of farm buildings and The Troops of The Squadron occupied these.

Looking back towards the bridge Pete could see the various tiers of defence surrounding it. As well as the Engineers who were attempting to prepare it for demolition, there was an Infantry Company dug in both sides of the river who he knew to be 7 Royal Anglian. More than a few of them would be known to guys in The Squadron. They recruited from the same area. There was also a Blowpipe Troop, Blowpipe being a shoulder fired anti-aircraft missile. It must take balls to stand out in the open or on the top of a vehicle and engage an approaching aircraft. On the other side of the bridge stood a recovery vehicle, its task would be to drag any casualties off the bridge. In a worst case scenario, it would simply be pushed into the river.

After a while the signal came to withdraw and The Troops leapfrogged back to and over the bridge. As Pete crossed Nick slowed down and shouted at two Military Policemen.

"OI KNOBHEAD", causing them to both turn and stare accusingly. The face of one of them burst into a grin as he recognised the offender. "EYUP BASTARD" he shouted back, "HOW YOU DOING"? Reaching out to shake hands. Unknown to everyone else they were cousins.

"When you've finished Nick, in your own time mate, we need to go" interrupted Pete.

"GET THAT FUCKING ROLLER SKATE OFF MY BRIDGE" screamed one of the engineers.

"FUCK OFF" Nick shouted back as he accelerated away.

As the last call sign crossed over, one of The Military Policemen handed over a written instruction to the engineer to blow the bridge.

Despite the fact that the Commanders of both The Engineers and the Infantry Company were senior to him in rank, only The Military Police Corporal had the right to order the bridge blown. That authority came directly from The Brigade Commander in the form of a CODEWORD.

To simulate its destruction it was marked with white mine tape.

As the defenders melted away, the Squadron made its way to the harbour area at PERCH.

CHAPTER SEVEN

THE RAID

From the harbour area at PERCH The Squadron made its way to a forested area which lay to the west of Deisel and was joined overnight by the combined Support Troops of all 4 squadrons. Together they fielded 20 Spartans and there was much speculation over what their mission would be. Support Troop concentrations at Regimental level occurred perhaps once a year and tended to involve range work. No one could remember them being deployed in this strength before.

The following day, all was revealed. The Squadron was to assist the four Support troops in a raid over the Weser.

Electronic Intelligence had detected the location of a Brigade Level command centre in a forest north east of Oberweser. This had been confirmed by The RAF who had conducted an aerial reconnaissance flight over the forest, identifying command vehicles, masts and helicopters.

The squadron would provide an escort for the raiding party, fire support on the objective and then secure a line of retreat afterwards.

An undefended bridge at Gieselwerder would be seized and held. There would then be a two and a half mile dash north to the objective with the various Troops within The Squadron deploying to prevent interference and provide force protection.

On approach, the raiding party would circumvent the location, breaking into it from the north. Each of the 4 Troops would clear the forest on a separate track, exiting from its southern edge. The whole force would then fall back across the river before the enemy could react.

As per the proposed plan, the bridge was secured by 5th Troop and led by 1st, the dash north began with appointed troops each deploying at junctions en-route. 2nd covered the approach road from the north at Oberweser with 3rd and 4th covering two roads which approached from the east on either side of a railway. These led from the town of Uslar which was known to be a major enemy location. Turning off the main road, which skirted the southern edge of the forest, 1st Troop took up fire positions to engage any enemy attempting to escape while the raiding party travelled further north to clear back down through it.

Almost immediately, 1st Troop detected activity along the eastern edge where camouflage was being torn down to reveal a number of light observation and command helicopters. They opened up with the co-axial machine guns, the drivers flashing their headlights to simulate gunfire. The Germans ignored this and scrambled, the aircraft bursting out in all directions at high speed.

They then turned their attention to the array of light vehicles which had broken cover from the southern edge and streamed towards them.

Jack laughed to himself as the umpires ran across their front trying to stop them, declaring them destroyed.

As they had raced down the approach track from the north, they had encountered what Digger supposed was the sentry post. Consisting of three guys in a ditch manning a Spandau, they didn't even attempt to engage the raiding party. At the next junction the track divided into 4, each one being taken by a separate troop. Towards the centre of the forest they came across groups of command vehicles and radio masts heavily concealed under nets which the sections fought through on foot.

He watched as the section of 4, working in pairs moved from vehicle to vehicle. At each point he would creep forward using the turret GPMG to support them. On their approach the enemy crews ran back to their vehicles, locking themselves inside. Digger wasn't sure if this was the S.O.P. for an attack but they offered no resistance and there was no evidence of a defence unit. In reality they were all doomed, with each vehicle being engaged by LAW and MAW systems, everyone would be killed. Given the array of masts and antennae this was an important installation with each member being a highly skilled and trained operator. Destroying this place would render the enemy dumb, blind and deaf. Others ran to vehicles and attempted to escape south but he knew that they would run into 1st Troop. He had never seen or witnessed so much gunfire and explosions and found it exhilarating. Regrouping at the southern end of the forest, the teams mounted up and as a group travelled past 1st Troop who were providing over-watch. The whole thing had been very quick and he could hear the guys in the back shouting excitedly to each other as the adrenalin continued to flow.

As the raiding party passed them, each FOX Troop in turn broke cover and followed them south, back across the Weser.

The whole thing had taken just under an hour.

They continued on to The Squadron hide at Deisel where, after allowing the guys time to decompress and calm down, a de-brief was conducted.

The raid was deemed a great success at Regiment and Brigade level. The dismounted raiding party had found it exciting but for the mounted FOX crews it had been a disappointment.

Following the de-brief, the group had broken up with the Support Troops returning to their separate Squadrons.

The Squadron itself moved to their hide location for the weekend, all military activity being curtailed, as demanded by the Local Government Authorities.

CHAPTER EIGHT

MIDDLE WEEKEND

The placing of bright yellow porta-loos, which were illuminated at night, defeated the point where it came to light and noise discipline, so these were relaxed. All the weapons were secured and the usual military practices stopped. It was just like camping.

The assigned location for the hide had been the forest west of the village of Beberbeck but SHQ decided otherwise and they had taken a position in a field screened from the road by trees. On the other side of the road was The GASTHAUS ZUM THIERGARTEN, a beer hall. The SQMS had struck a deal with the proprietor giving The Squadron exclusive use of it for that night with a promise that they would be left alone after that. The owners of course had been here before and realised that they could make a lot of money.

A deal was also struck with the farmer who owned the field, who was compensated with a considerable amount of petrol.

"I wouldn't put that crap in my vehicles" thought The SQMS at the time but the farmer was happy.

He also knew that The British Army would compensate any damage to his land and buildings and there was an old barn and some gates which needed to be replaced.

The rest of the day was spent tidying away the wagons and getting cleaned up for the evening's activities "over the road".

The beerhall was pretty typical with those all over Northern Germany, rows of long tables and benches with a raised platform at one end. There was dark, carved wood everywhere, on the walls, the roof beams, the bar, serving hatches and individual stalls. Pete noticed that part of the "gingerbread" carving consisted of swastika emblems, and he could just imagine the walls draped with banners and a portrait of The Fuhrer or The Kaiser at the end of the hall.

The fare was the usual, Jagerschnitzel, Bratwurst, buckets of chips and huge steins of the local Lager served by girls dressed in the traditional costume of Tyrolean milkmaids. Pete found them quite attractive and it amazed him that a people so full of life and zeal could also be capable of the atrocities that occurred in the forties. In fairness though, The British Empire had committed genocide and incarcerated whole populations in its efforts to make the world atlas pink in colour. The Germans, as usual, had unfortunately just been a bit more efficient at it.

As the night evolved, the traditional "Umpah" music played by little fat men in Lederhosen gave way to songs from the individual tables. They increased in noise and vulgarity as the different Troops competed, with Boot Troop winning as usual. Making up a third of The Squadron, it wasn't surprising really.

During the course of the evening, The Officers made their way into the main hall to the jeers of the gathered men.

They had secured a couple of rooms upstairs which had allowed them to take advantage of the bathrooms where they were able to wash, shave and change into clean uniforms. They would of course change back into their soiled kit when the exercise continued.

They had also been able to acquire a private dining room where they had eaten and drunk separately to the men. Visiting the main hall was merely a gesture of solidarity which was appreciated by them. Charlie had felt quietly uneasy about not socializing with his Troop and had contented himself with paying for their dinner. After an obligatory half hour, they retired again, The Squadron Leader giving The SSM an assertive nod of the head, making his thoughts known. The SSM in turn looked around the room and thought to himself that another hour will do it and he would wind things down.

As the tables emptied, they delighted the serving girls by leaving them large tips as compensation for their services and putting up with a certain amount of well-intentioned abuse.

Back at the harbour area most of The Squadron went quietly to their beds but inevitably a few remained awake to drink further and carouse until eventually being told to "FUCKING SHUT UP".

Charlie decided not to return and made use of one of the beds in the rented rooms. He was surprised that only a few of The Officers thought to do so.

The next morning, at a reasonable time, The Squadron Leader and SSM made a tour of the location. He had informed everyone the day before that it would happen and was pleased that despite the obvious sore heads, everyone on parade had washed and shaved and that the individual Troop areas were squared away. Boots had been cleaned and berets brushed. He was especially pleased by the efforts of 1st Troop, himself having been its former commander before acquiring his Majority and ascending to command of The Squadron. He was further delighted to receive an invitation to "Sunday lunch" by the Troop.

2nd Troop had seemingly sorted themselves out as well having endured his wrath concerning their poor performance in the O.P. line. As punishment he had decreed that they alone should provide the sentries the night before, missing out on events.

The days schedule was that vehicle maintenance and refuelling should be carried out in the morning with the cleaning of all the weapons including The RARDEN in the afternoon.

That would leave time for them to work out their "routines" for the concert party later that evening. Having agreed with the Gasthaus that they would be left to cater for their regular clientele the second night, The Squadron endeavoured to entertain themselves.

As soon as it was dark the guys gathered around the bonfire which the farmer had consented to and had even supplied firewood for. To his delight, a working party had been provided which had cleared his property of vast amounts of pallets and wooden fencing.

Beer was supplied by The SQMS as was meat which was cooked on a 25 gallon drum, split and mounted on a trellis. The guys though had been drinking their own supplies throughout the day and his sales were down. At the start of the scheme the new Brigade commander had decreed that it would be a "Dry" exercise. The Colonel of The Regiment however had commented that "The cavalry had NEVER had a dry exercise". He conceded though that although alcohol was banned, Beer could still be consumed. This had been largely ignored, in fact Pete himself had been drinking from a 2 litre bottle of Coke liberally laced with Bacardi all week.

Once everyone had eaten their share of the barbeque and indulged in some Beer, the concert party began. Each Troop had to provide some form of entertainment which involved the participation of the whole Troop.

Most Troops performed popular songs that were in the charts at the time with choreographed dance routines, 1st

did a cover of "summer loving" from "Grease" with Nick Shields playing Olivia Newton John and Charlie playing John Travolta

4th re-enacted a sketch from "It ain't alf ot mum".

Best performance went to 5th Troop though with their cover of "I'm going to wash that man right out of my hair" from "South Pacific". They even went to the bother of turning ferns collected from the forest into grass skirts and wearing 2 mess tins on a boot lace draped around their necks to simulate bikini tops.

As the night went on things became more and more surreal ending with the ceremony of everyone throwing their week old, dirty and smelly underwear onto the fire.

"It's just as well we're doing this" commented the young Cornet Hulme to everyone in earshot. "My new girlfriend would be horrified if I returned with dirty underwear for her to wash, she's ever so funny about such things,"

You just don't divulge information like this in The Army. In a short time, a large part of The Squadrons dirty underwear
had been hidden in Cornet Hulme's laundry bag for return to The UK.

The following morning was a Sunday and a Church Parade was planned for late morning. In the meantime, broken bodies and sore heads recovered.

At the appointed time the Squadron paraded in front of the makeshift altar which consisted of a trestle table draped in a Squadron flag with two guidons behind.

The Regimental Padre addressed the parade…"Good morning gentlemen and welcome to this, my first church parade as your Padre".

"Don't worry, I'm not going to expect you to sing, I've heard your singing and you're crap".

This brought forward a combined chorus of laughs and chuckles.

"Instead, I'm going to read the words of the late Reverent Leslie Skinner that we might all reflect on them. Many of these events took place not so far from where we are now stood".   The Reverent Leslie Skinner had joined The Unit as it's Padre in Normandy in 1944 and was one of the most revered men of a generation which was held in awe by those that followed. As well as his normal pastoral administrations he took it upon himself to take a very personal interest in the welfare of the men.

Wherever possible he made it his duty to locate the remains of any man who was killed, provide him with a proper funeral and record the details so that the body could be later interred and buried with due respect and recognition. He also wrote to the family and loved ones if at all possible.

Together with a small number of volunteers he also recovered the charred and mummified bodies of the crews who were killed in the tanks. He didn't think that surviving members should witness the carnage. How could they be expected to serve on knowing what their fate might be?

Some of the passages came from letters home to his family and others as part of his own biography. Very often the sights, smells and duties he had to perform had made him physically sick.

The congregation listened in complete silence many showing their feelings in their demeanour. It was a sobering experience.

Although he had read the accounts himself, Pete couldn't help but be moved.

After a respectful silence to allow the guys to reflect he said "One of the most profound statements that The Reverent Skinner made was…There are no atheists on the battlefield".

"We will now recite The Lord's Prayer".

This was followed by the singing of The National Anthem before the accompanying Roman Catholic Padre was introduced and a part of the congregation was invited to take communion.

Not a religious person himself, Pete was surprised at the number who approached the Padre. One of the Squadrons recruited in Northern Ireland and he would expect a good response from them but not so much from this Squadron

As the Padres prepared to move to the next location, a vehicle appeared which was known throughout The Yeomanry This was a civilian Range Rover painted in the green and black scheme of The Army and fitted for radio. Its occupants included Gerald Grosvenor, Duke of Westminster and reportedly the richest man in England. He was also The O.C. of a Squadron in a sister
Yeomanry regiment. Making good use of "a day off", he was visiting friends amongst other units in the area.

An enigmatic character, he was universally respected throughout the Army and was a keen promoter of The Territorial Army. A number of outlandish stories which related to him were always being bandied about including…

He had wanted to purchase CVR(T)'s for his Squadron but had been refused by The M.O.D.

He had once, during a particularly hard and wet exercise, arranged for a personal helicopter to transfer his officers and himself to a country hotel for a bath and hot meal.

Whether these stories were true or not, they certainly reflected the eccentric character of The Yeomanry.

Pete and Jack now had other issues to ponder though, namely the "Sunday Lunch" to which The Squadron Leader had been invited.

Two 6 foot tables and folding chairs had been acquired from ADMIN Troop and the meal was made from the contents of a 10 man Ration Pack. The menu was…

STARTER
  Mock Turtle Soup.
MAIN COURSE
  Steamed Steak and Kidney Pudding, Tinned Vegetables, tinned potatoes and Gravy (Oxtail Soup).
DESERT
  Fruit Cake.

Hock was provided with the meal and Jagermeister for the toasts, with cigars for those who desired them.

The meal went well with Pete proposing The Loyal Toast, Jack proposing a toast to The Regiment and The Squadron Leader reciprocating with a toast to 1st Troop.

Once the proceedings were finished, Pete volunteered Windy and Paddy to help him return the plates and cutlery to the Gasthaus.

During the party at the Gasthaus on the first night he had approached the Lady owner who had supplied the plates, cutlery, alcohol and cigars. He had accompanied her into the back parlour to negotiate and on return, they had been greeted with whistles, catcalls and jeering by the closest table. The owner who was middle aged but still quite attractive blushed and Pete was convinced that she was actually flattered rather than embarrassed.

Entering through the kitchen, Pete told the guys where to put the borrowed items and turned to face the owner. Conversing in perfect German, he thanked her and she asked him how the lunch had gone. Indicating to the other two that they could leave, he continued to hold her in conversation, sensing that they had made some sort of a connection.

After a few minutes she asked him if he would like a drink and automatically turning to the bar, realised that she was instead moving up the stairs to the apartment above.

Following her into the parlour, he stood behind her as she poured 2 shots of Apfelkorn, a form of schnapps. He didn't really like Schnapps but didn't want to offend.

Looking over her shoulder he could sense that his presence was exiting her and that she was aware that he was looking down her cleavage. He reached around to put his hands on her stomach, pulling her towards him and she responded by putting down the glasses and reaching behind to fondle him through his trousers.

Sometime later, Ron Andrews watched as Pete walked through the harbour area. He had seen the three of them leave and only two return. He also remembered the way Pete had interacted with the landlady the other evening. As he passed Ron asked "Have you had a pleasant afternoon Corporal Wood"? To which he replied "Very pleasant thankyou Sar'nt Major".

After a few seconds he called after him "Pete".

"Yes Sir"?

There was a pause.

"Nothing mate, carry on".

"Sir" he affirmed and kept walking.

As a rule, when he had his hat on, he would never address anyone junior by their first name, never mind call them "mate".   But he knew Pete's history, their paths had crossed before but neither of them would ever disclose the covert nature of their work years before.

When he returned to the Troop, most of them were sleeping it off. Windy was reading his "Wheels of Terror" and looked up knowingly.

Getting no response from Pete he returned to his book.

CHAPTER NINE

THE M.S.R.

Later that afternoon, The Squadron Leader returned from an O group at RHQ, which was located in the nearby forest, and convened one himself. As they gathered around Charlie, The Troop listened intently. The routine of the hide was starting to get boring.

Pete observed the faces of the group, taking in the fact that they nearly all had "Charlie Bronson" type moustaches. It was because of this that they were known within the Squadron as "The Mexicans". Moustaches were very trendy in the British Army at the moment, it had been sideburns during The Napoleonic Wars. Now it was moustaches. Pete tended to favour both. Paddy was desperately trying to eat a curry whilst fighting off two others who kept making attacks on it with their "racing spoons". Everyone in the army had a racing spoon, carried in a pocket on their left arm, nobody's dinner was safe. There was a constant search
for the ultimate spoon, which had a small handle and a large ladle. It was the equivalent of the quest for The Holy Grail.

"The Squadron is to establish a patrol base at a location about 60 miles from here in order to control and protect an M.S.R. From midnight we will be on 10 minutes notice to move and it is expected that we will be required to be "on task" by 06:00".

Some of the group showed a genuine interest but those who knew better were recognisable by the resigned looks on their faces.

"The Troop is now on 30 minutes notice, we'll travel in the order we are in now, and the route is marked on my map". The last part he directed at the other commanders.

"The locals will be awake by then and so we will show all our lights, any questions". He looked around the group, George as usual had something to add.

"It's Monday morning and the locals will still have their "sleepy heads" on. They know the roads, we don't, so just be aware of them".

"Anything else? Ok, let's get sorted while it's still light". By 02:00 The Squadron was on the move, South West through The Beberbeck Forest and then North West towards Paderborn. The Brigade locations in the forested areas were all obvious, indicated by the dozens of illuminated "porta-loos". There was movement everywhere but they seemed to be the only unit actually on the road. Pete thought that it must be because they had been tasked with establishing the M.S.R.?

Because his wagon was last in the packet Pete allowed his concentration to wander, thinking about the events of the previous day.

Marta had proved to be a very competent lover, why was it that he was attracted to older women? His thoughts drifted to others, June Andrews in particular. Ron Andrews the PSI SSM and himself had been working for BRIXMIS out of the town of Bunde at the time. Ron had been on the other side of the border for a while and they had struck up a relationship which he had at first been slow to recognise. Despite warnings from other members of the unit and their partners, it had developed into an affair. These things happened all too often in The Army when couples were separated for long periods of time. There were many reasons, boredom being the main one. As a rule they fizzled out and most marriages survived. It had been June who had ended it, being older and having a more practical outlook on life, she had told him that she was happy in her relationship with Ron and that she had children to consider. In a way, it had come as something of a relief to him but he would always think of her with fondness.

As far as he knew, Ron had never discovered about the affair. He thought about their earlier encounter. Pete had been given the impression that Ron had wanted to bring up something important, but had then changed his mind. Perhaps he was reading too much into it?

Bypassing Paderborn they drove on through the town of Rhede to Warendorf, their destination. Leaving the main road, they crossed The Ems canal before turning again into a large cleared area which was a patchwork of grassed squares divided by cinder tracks. The derelict building at the entrance had a definite military appearance about it, almost like a guardhouse and the site was enclosed in a wire fence with a perimeter road?

Pete was immediately aware of its previous function, every town in German had possessed one, even if the local population had denied that they knew of its existence. This had been a forced labour camp, the occupants collected from all over occupied Europe would have been used in local factories, mines or on the land. The conditions varied from camp to camp depending on the skill level of its inhabitants. Not "Death Camps" as such but in the lower status ones, many had died of disease or malnutrition.

Some units were already in occupancy, a Field Ambulance, Provost Platoon and REME Recovery Squadron amongst them.

In one corner sat a Puma which caught the professional eye of Paddy.

The workhorse of the Joint Helicopter Force in BAOR, he noticed that it had been fitted with dust filters on the engine inlets. It had obviously been used previously in The Middle East, most likely on Cyprus he thought. The Spartans of Boot Troop sat with it with the guys themselves grouped around two figures in flying suits.

1st Troop was soon made aware of what their role would be for at least the next couple of days. An MSR had been established which included the B64 between Paderborn and Munster. In reality it would have been the autobahn which ran parallel but The German authorities didn't want The British Army playing on its motorways. The Squadron would be responsible for a section of what was now designated as route HORSE. Their area of responsibility began at Rheda which was STALLION, their own location was STEED and Munster at the northern end MARE. The 5 sabre troops would rotate as patrols of 2 vehicles anti clockwise taking it in turns to form a reserve. Boot Troop would be the Rapid Reaction Force and were at that time, getting up to speed with drills on The Puma.

Pete studied his map, picking out all the garrison towns which were so familiar to him.

East of his location was a wooded ridge shaped like a bow with Bielefeld in the centre, Osnabruck on its northern tip and Paderborn on the southern one.

On the outer side of the bow were Detmold, Herford and Bunde with Munster, Hamm and Dortmund on the inside. This ridge was the final defence line before The Rhine. Dortmund was the home of most of the Medium Field Artillery Regiments and had always been known as "Gunners Ghetto".

He thought about the mind numbing tedium of patrolling the MSR for days and watched Boot Troop enviously as they practiced deploying from the Puma.

"John Boy" looked around his troop as it split into groups. The Puma could carry up to 16 troops and he had divided The Troop into 4 chalks of 7 men each. 2 guys had decided to drop out, one through a leg injury acquired playing murder ball the previous day and the other because he wasn't happy about abseiling from the helicopter.

The two loadmasters took 2 chalks each and talked them through the drills. Covering first the actions on an emergency or forced landing, they then went on to loading and unloading using their webbing to mark out the seat positions on the ground before practicing on the helicopter itself. They also learnt the 3 hand signals which would be used to indicate whether they would be deployed by landing, hovering or on the rope. Finally, they were taught how to mount the rope and slide down it properly.

It was his first time with The Puma, having used Scout and Wessex in Ulster. The Scout had been fun with only the pilot and section commander having seats, the commanders' facing the rear. The 4 other guys sat on the floor facing outwards with their feet on the skids. AAC pilots tended to be Corporals, a lot of them ex Chieftain Drivers for some reason, and they flew below tree top level, hopping over walls and hedges and skimming under power lines. Having skids, they tended to slide across the ground before rising again. The section were expected to dismount whilst it was still moving, if you were slow, it could mean a long drop.

The Wessex was entirely different, being both slow and large. Because it was RAF the pilots were all commissioned officers and it tended to fly above 500 meters, freefalling down at the last moment to deploy its' troops. It took forever for it to build up enough energy to take off again and so was very vulnerable.

The chalks formed up waiting for The Puma to run through its start-up routine. At a signal from the "loadies" they approached both sides as practiced and it lifted off. After about a quarter of a mile it landed again and the 2 chalks debussed assuming an "all round defence" posture. It returned with the other 2 chalks and they carried out the same procedure. The first lift were already formed up in two lines and at the signal remounted. the second deployment was at the hover and the third from about 10 meters down the rope. This last one was back at the harbour area and The Puma immediately headed off to nearby RAF Gutersloh for some lunch and to re-fuel.

"John Boy" decided that 4 vehicle sections would provide the airborne element of the Quick Reaction Force, the others would remain with The Spartans as a ground unit.

The soul destroying routine of patrolling the MSR went on for two days, a single circuit taking up to 2 hours at a time before returning to the harbour area. Only three events occurred to break 1st Troops' tedium, one of them not set up by the umpires though.

On the first afternoon it was declared that the bridge at Schulze-Vohren had been destroyed by aircraft and a diversion had to be established. Although the civilian traffic continued as normal, all military vehicles had to be moved into a harbour area whist The Royal Engineer constructed an off ramp to carry traffic on to a parallel side road. As the MSR was only operating in one direction it proved easier than it might have been although the recovery of a number of casualties caused problems. It helped to break the monotony though. On the second day Pete and Charlie

were tasked to investigate the report of a SOXMIS vehicle which was observing the activity on the MSR.

When Germany had been divided into four zones of occupation after The Second World War, it was agreed that each of the occupying powers would establish a military liaison unit. Travelling in especially marked vehicle with diplomatic immunity, they would travel throughout Germany to observe their opponents activities. The Soviet unit was designated as SOXMIS, an abbreviation of Soviet Military Mission. There was however thirteen areas in The British sector which were off limits by agreement. All British troops in Germany carried an information card giving a contact phone number at Herford and a picture of the diplomatic plate. They were obliged to inform Herford of any sighting.

They located the vehicle east of Telgte where there was a bend in the MSR with a side road leading into a wooded area. This allowed the observers a clear view back down the route for about 5 miles.

As they dismounted and approached the vehicle, Pete briefed everyone on the niceties which they were obliged to observe. Charlie was relieved, as this was a situation he wasn't comfortable with.

"They have diplomatic immunity so they can't be physically interfered with and this isn't a restricted area, so we don't have the right to take their cameras or equipment, basically, they are just truck spotters".

The two guys paid them the slightest of attention and then carried on, Pete noticing the very expensive German camera which was mounted on a tri-pod, as he moved around them taking mental notes of what he could see.

After about ten minutes George came on the air about a situation which was developing just east of the harbour area and Charlie declared that he was responding.

"You carry on here Corporal Wood, we'll meet up back at the harbour area".

"Right Boss" he replied noticing with pleasure that Nick took Charlie's departure as the que for getting a brew on. Sipping his coffee, Pete walked to the front of the Opel Senator, taking in the blacked out windows with small round sections which could be removed to accommodate cameras. He knew that it would be no normal senator, fitted with all sorts of gadgets including a blackout switch and a rallying style roll cage. He also knew that if he had to give chase, the 4 litre Jag engine in his FOX wouldn't be enough to keep up. The car was relatively clean but the yellow and red diplomatic plate with its unique number was covered in mud. Deciding that he needed a piss he cleaned it off revealing the number 36.

He noticed that they became very interested when certain types of vehicles passed down the road and just chatted between themselves the rest of the time. They paid no interest in The FOX whatsoever which said a lot about their opinion of it.

After about an hour they packed up and without even acknowledging him, headed in the direction of the town.

Taking the time to check out a roadside burger bar on the way they returned to the harbour area where, taking his webbing and "gat", Pete made his way to the tents of the Provost unit.

On entry, he knew that he would receive some sort of comment from the "Monkies".

"Hello, it's the SAS lads, what can we do for you mate"?"

By SAS they meant "Saturdays and Sundays", a common nickname for The Territorials.

"Here to make a SOXMIS report mate" Pete replied, taking in the furnishings in the command post.

"Take a seat, I'll just get up the report form for Herford he said, bringing up the correct screen on the monitor.

The Corporal typed as Pete narrated, first giving his name, rank, number and unit.

"At 13:00 hrs today I had contact with a SOXMIS vehicle, numbered 36 which was a green Opel Senator converted for covert ops. They were observing vehicle activity on the B64 east of Telgte and seemed interested in MLRS and TRACKED RAPIER. There was 2 operatives, dressed as East German officers but talking in Russian. They wore Captains insignia, but judging by their ages were most likely senior NCO's. At approximately 14:00 hours they drove north towards the town of Telgte".

"Excellent", The Corporal responded as Pete caught movement in the entrance and his eyes met those of a huge MP Staff Sergeant with a bright, pink, pock marked face. He was cradling a GPMG.

"Fucking hell it's RAMBO" declared someone.

"BOON ASS, how you doing mate"? Pete exclaimed happily.

"Pete, how they hanging mate, been a while" he replied as he extended a huge hand. "What's occurring"?

"SOXMIS sighting, usual shit".

"Still see any of the Bunde mob"? He enquired.

"No mate, although, do you remember Ron Andrews, he's a PSI with my TA unit"?

"BRIXMIS, had a fit wife"? He asked.

"That's the one, bit warry isn't it"? Pete asked, gesturing at the machine gun.

"Bin picking kit up all week, got a tent full around the back. Who loses a fucking Jimpy"?

Boon Ass had been on "White Mice" operations at Bunde when Pete had been attached to SOXMIS there. It was amazing that in The Army you could meet people after many years and just drop back into a conversation as if it were only yesterday.

They spent a further half hour reminiscing before Pete made his apologies and returned to the wagon. He noticed that the rest of The Troop had returned and over a brew and an "egg banjo", caught up on earlier events.

At the time when reports of the SOXMIS had come in, 1st Troop had been in reserve. While Charlie and Pete had dealt with that, George and Sharpie had been tasked to investigate reports of a large group of people moving on foot towards the MSR from the direction of Wesselmann to the north.

Between Wesselmann and the MSR was a bridge which crossed The Ems. It consisted of a road bridge with a separate one supporting a cycle route and footpath. George decided to block the road section and direct the mob onto the lesser bridge where they could be contained. He parked his own wagon on the nearside of the canal and told Sharpie to take his off to one side where he could cover the bridge with his co-axial machine gun.

Dismounting the lads, they shepherded the crowd onto the bridge and he was approached by a woman who appeared to be in charge. Amongst the women in the group were several small children and pets.

As she approached she pleaded to him.
"Can you help us please, we're from the garrison at Osnabruck, we've been evacuated and are trying to reach Rheindahlen. Our bus has broken down and we have been walking for hours, we are all very tired, hungry and thirsty"? At that, a number of them started wailing and sobbing which set off the kids and dogs

"Bloody Hell!" Thought George, "do I look like a fucking social worker"?
Judging by her accent and appearance, he guessed that she was probably an Officers wife. "I'm well over my head here" he thought. The rest of The Troop smirked at his obvious discomfort.

"Please stay calm Ma'am, I will get you help"

"This is one for The Lad" George thought and immediately called him up for support.

Amongst the crowd was a group of Officers with clip boards who appeared to be scrutinizing him. As the crowd got louder and the kids and pets more distressed, he constantly looked at his watch, hoping that Charlie would get there soon.

To his relief Charlie appeared and was made aware of the situation.

Calling over the group's leader he told her, "Can you get your people into the shade of those trees please, I will arrange some food and water and medical treatment if you need it".

"Corporal Sharp, take your wagon down the road, see if you can find their transport and arrange for its recovery if possible".

"Briggs, Flaherty, check everyone's I.D's as they come off the bridge and search the prams".

"Sir" they both affirmed.

"Hardy, Miller, break out some water and whatever available food you can find".

"Give the brats some boiled sweets, it might shut them up" was Georges contribution.

"Don't you fucking DARE!" he grunted at Jim Hardy as he made to distribute some of the bottles of beer, I don't share my beer with anyone!!"

Over the radio Jack announced that he had found the transport and that REME were attending and sometime later it appeared, escorted by Jack.

To Jacks pleasure it turned out to be an old Army Bedford of the type which he had travelled to school in for many years.

With the refugees fed, watered and rested, they were sent on their way.

"Obviously looking to terrorise someone else" thought George.

As the afternoon wore on, more and more elements of B Squadron started to appear and The Troop realised that they might finally get another task.

CHAPTER TEN

CONTAINMENT

With the arrival of B Squadron, responsibility for the MSR was handed over and A Squadron went into reserve. They were to provide a containment force if an airborne attack on the MSR occurred. The open fields which ranged along both sides of the route provided plenty of options for a landing zone. It wasn't expected that an attack would occur during dark and so The Squadron carried out roving patrols at dawn the following day, traveling up and down the parallel roads. SHQ and ADMIN remained at Warendorf with the individual troops returning there to replenish.

Boredom began to set in again with the guys convinced that The Brigade Commander, as before, had put them on the back shelf. Left to their own devices, the Troops found night locations close to Gasthofs but still stood to at dawn on the second day as was their nature. They had just stood down when the warning order came through.

Brigade believed that an assault would occur at RAF Gutersloh and The Squadron moved on two parallel roads to take up pre-designated locations. Ranged clockwise around the expected landing zone, 4 Troops were placed to form a ring with 5th and Support in reserve. They would move as the situation dictated.

Automatically taking up a position North West of the airfield, 1st Troops' vehicle commanders got together to discuss probable scenarios.

The northern edge of the airfield was bordered by a busy main road and it was accepted that it would not be included in the exercise. Along the southern edge ran The Ems with only a few minor bridges, the western border had a road which ran directly to the MSR but no access onto it unless they crashed through the boundary fence. The eastern border had a number of gated exits and they reasoned that that would be the direction of any attempted breakout.

SHQ obviously came to the same conclusion and placed Support and 5th Troops to the east. The resident RAF Regiment Squadron with Scorpion and Spartan would deploy within the perimeter fence to protect the facilities backed up by a RAPIER battery.

Two tracks ran from the western fence to the road leading to the MSR and beyond it was a wooded area which 1st Troop took up position in. From here they were able to observe the road right down to where it crossed The Ems and the tempting Gasthaus on the other side of the bridge.

Paddy was in his element as he watched the constant stream of Tornados with their "shark fin" profiles which took off directly over their location at the end of the runway. He was an aero engineer with Rolls Royce back in the real world and although he was one of the most junior troopers in the unit, he was actually one of the most qualified professionally and probably the best paid. Tornado was relatively new in service and proclaimed itself to be a Multi-Role Combat Aircraft. Paddy knew that it was actually a Jack of all trades and master of none. The air defence variant was underpowered and struggled to keep up with the older models deployed in the Combat Air Patrols over Europe. The ground attack variant was no better when it had a full payload but was uniquely capable of carrying a certain area denial weapon which made it ideal for attacking airfields in East Germany. With some encouragement from The Troop, Charlie agreed that it would be necessary to occasionally send a vehicle across the canal to liaise with 4th Troop on their southern flank. The Gasthaus with its concealed car park at the rear was ideal and the four vehicles took it in turns to make the patrol. On immediate notice to move, the wagons were ready to crash out and the crews contented themselves with lying on the engine decks or snoozing in their seats..

"STAND TO". The shouted command echoed around the hide, startling everyone who, to a man, stared at Pete.

Charlie gave him a confused, half asleep look from his turret. "The flying has stopped, they're not going to allow an air assault onto an active airfield" Pete explained. Everyone became aware of the strange calm after hours of roaring jet engines.

"MOUNT UP" roared George, sending everyone into a state of activity. It took less than a minute for everyone to take their crew positions and fire up the engines.

Over the air came the words…"Hello all stations this is Zero, Stand to, out". They had obviously come to the same conclusion.

Charlie became aware of a faint drumming sound like the air pressure in his ears changing and he removed his helmet to locate its direction.

From the south east 2 specs which grew into 2 Phantom jets in Luftwaffe colours screamed across the airfield, followed immediately by another 2 from the south. Their paths took them directly over the Rapier Battery. Within a minute the distinctive sound of helicopter blades beating the air could be heard to the east.

Using their binoculars, all four commanders had a fleeting glimpse of a line of Sea Stallions, descending onto the far end of the main runway before their view was obscured by trees and buildings.

The radio waves were suddenly full of sighting reports, sent in clear, which gave 1st Troop an immediate understanding of the situation.

The 6 helicopters had each deployed 2 of the small, agile Weasels which SHQ had encountered at the start of the exercise before streaming away at low level in all directions. These threaded their way through a maze of hardened aircraft bunkers before exiting through a gate in the perimeter fence. Believing that they had gone to ground, the Spartans of The RAF Regiment had debussed and were clearing the bunkers on foot with their Scorpions stalking their prey. The track that the raiding party had taken led to a main road less than 2 miles away which would in turn allow them to bisect the MSR just north of Rheda.

The Squadron immediately started moving towards the MSR with each Troop deciding on their own route. SHQ were on the ball and directed 4th to block the main road where it crossed The Ems by traversing along a parallel road from their location in the village of Niemann.

Charlie, pre-empting SHQ's instructions started moving south over The Ems, passing behind 4th to block the next crossing at Nord-Rheda.

On leaving the airfield the raiders had crossed a junction with woods on two sides which just happened to be Support Troop's location. Although they weren't prepared for an ambush, the umpires gave them 1 kill with the rest of the raiders pushing through at high speed and Support Troop in pursuit. 2nd, 3rd and 5th who had been deployed to the east of the airfield, also moved south creating a screen to the east of the raiders. As they turned west onto the main road, the enemy crossed The Maas river onto a peninsula with The Maas on one side and The Ems on the other. This created a funnel which opened out to the south. With 4th holding the bridge over the Ems ahead and 3rd following up to close the one over The Maas behind them, they were forced to travel south. The terrain between the two rivers was a maze of woods and ditch edged fields crossed by a spider's web of tracks. Having to navigate through it slowed them down considerably. Moving down the eastern side of the funnel, 5th seized the next bridge over The Maas.

The southern, open end of the funnel was enclosed by a railway embankment and when 2nd closed the 2 tunnels under it, the raiders were effectively trapped.

Under the control of SHQ, the 6 Troops started to compress the size of the funnel, securing each junction as they went. Because of the ditches and fence lines around the fields, The Weasels were unable to use their off-road capability to find a gap in the cordon. After a number of engagements which involved taking and inflicting casualties, they were eventually trapped in the corner of a wood with tracks on 3 sides and an open field on the last.

1st Troop, moving in from their bridge over The Ems found themselves in a tree line. Across the open field in front of

them a number of the toad like vehicles could be seen forming up. They allowed them to get half way across before engaging them, with the survivors popping smoke and retreating into the wood again. Ron Andrews was there again with his armband and after consultation declared that George's vehicle had been lost, much to his disgust.

It was left to Boot Troop to clear the wood and capture the remaining raiders. While this was happening, 1st Troop got a brew on and had something to eat as was their usual routine.

CHAPTER ELEVEN

ENDEX

Following the "brew", with the engagement obviously over, Charlie pulled the Troop back from the treeline to line up on a track. It wasn't long before the order came for all Troop Leaders to RV at SHQ's location.

On his return, he briefed everyone about what was expected to happen next. RHQ believed that things were starting to wind down, with a lack of tasks being allotted by Brigade. The Squadron was tasked with establishing a picket line based on The Ems Canal to protect the MSR from any attempted assault from the north-east. As the FEBA was some way to the east this wasn't considered likely. 1st Troop were to return to the area of Brocke Muhle which was where The Gasthaus they had frequented the day before was located and observe the bridge over The Ems. It took less than half an hour to reach it and they established a hide in a coppice on the opposite side of the road to the Gasthaus. From here they were able to monitor the bridge, a mere 250 meters away .One of the vehicles was set up for the O.P. and the usual routine established. It was decided that only one person would be needed in the turret with another as a sentry at the entrance to the coppice. Charlie explained that they would be in position until ENDEX was announced the following morning, at which time the Squadron would regroup at Warendorf.

The bivvies were set up and the hide made as comfortable as possible, Charlie deciding that they would make a "camp curry" using all the compo available and consume a fair amount of the Herforder Pils. Anything left would be stored for return to The UK. He also ordered that all the personal weapons be secured, it was time for a period of "decompression". It wasn't thought that the landowner would appreciate a bonfire and so they improvised by placing beacons inside a pile of timber.

The hide became a laid back affair with the "Stag" being changed every hour and the atmosphere quickly subduing as exhaustion took over. As the beer flowed, each man revealed his motivation for joining although, in a few cases a lot of the facts were kept back. The reasons were pretty typical with some having previously served in the regulars, the cadets, or merely wanting to obtain a driving licence. Their characters were all different as well. Being a "citizen army" they reflected British society as a whole. Some had done time, committed low key crimes and even "done drugs" previously. They came from all social classes and had varying levels of education. Their personal income and responsibilities weren't always comparable with their position or status within The Troop either

None of this mattered though. The uniform they wore was a great equalizer and they had formed a bond. They were mates and although they were unaware of it, when they met again decades later, they would still be mates. This was one of the enigmas of military life.

The radio message, when it came through, was met with mixed feelings by the guys.

"Hello all stations this is Zero, ENDEX, I say again ENDEX. Move to STEED now. Papa 10 and Papa 40 acknowledge over".

"Papa 10, Roger, over", "Papa 40, Roger, over" came the replies.

"Zero, roger out".

Over the next few hours The Regiment came together at Warendorf and were briefed. They were to move in Squadron packets back to the rail head at Brunswick, except the land party who would travel independently to The Hook of Holland via Munster.

Whilst waiting for their appointed departure time, the crews sorted out their wagons, removing the cam-nets and external kit and fuelling up for the 130 mile journey.

At the last minute, it was announced that all the weapons would be returning with the land party and an armed escort would be needed. This meant that they had to be cleaned first and a guard detail formed. There was very few takers, the attraction of a night "down the town" with their mates in Brunswick was too much and in the end, one guy from each Troop had to be "volunteered".

The road move itself proved to be pretty straight forward with a 25 mile run to Rheda to pick up the A2 which took them all the way to Brunswick, bypassing to the north of Hannover. At the gap in the hills called The Porta Westfallica they saw the impressive statue of Kaiser Wilhelm standing on the hill above The Weser. Jack could remember it, when as a kid, he had visited relatives stationed at nearby Minden.

The controlled move took the best part of 5 hours and as soon as they arrived they started prepping the vehicles for loading into their shipping containers. As well as removing all external storage, a DEFRA inspector, specifically flown out for the task, insisted that all food stuffs be removed as well as the cam-nets and rolls of hessian. He then personally supervised the decontamination of each vehicle especially the wheels and suspension. There was a scare at that time about a beetle which was devastating the potato crop in Germany. The worry was that it would be carried to The UK.

The preparations took the best part of that evening and into the following day after which the guys were moved by coach to Northampton Barracks at Wolfenbuttel. Accommodation had been found for both the senior ranks and Officers in their respective messes with everyone else having to make do with their sleeping bags and the floor of the gym. With over 100 guys and only 3 toilets, sinks and showers, it should have been a nightmare but they were so tired that they hardly noticed. While the rest slept, Jack got washed and dressed and decided to take a walk.

He had lived here in the early 70's as a kid and was curious as to what had changed since then? He remembered attending the trampoline club at the gym and the NAAFI shop next to it and also the cinema where all the "Brats" would spend their pocket money at the matinee on a Saturday morning. Like all German Barracks it was impressive, with 4 story accommodation blocks arranged around a central square and approached through an arch. Above the TOC H, on the top floor, had been his classroom, there being no room at the actual school which was about a quarter of a mile away. The internal parade square was now grass with a large flower bed at one end. For decades he had heard claims made by the hundreds of soldiers stationed there about hearing the

Screams of men and the sounds of medical instruments during the night.

Rumour had it that the flower bed concealed the entrance to an underground hospital which had been sealed up by The American troops who had liberated it in 1945?

Germany was full of such ghost stories he thought. Passing through the front gates with their giant German eagle still visible and an uninterested guard, he crossed the road and walked along Elbinger Strasse, past the school and then down Breslauer Strasse where they had lived for a while. Unlike most garrison towns over here, the married quarters were mixed in with the local housing. This, along with the fact that The Regiment here was isolated from the rest of B.A.O.R. made it a popular posting. The pub, Danziger Eck was still there, and still frequented by the Turkish labourers who were granted work permits he noticed. A stroll up Jahnstrasse brought him to the married quarters at Am Atzumer Busch. He had also lived here before going to boarding school in Dortmund and tried to remember his friends and girlfriends who had lived in the surrounding houses. So many memories he thought, before going up the hill, back to the camp.   Lunch was taken in the cookhouse, which they had to themselves because the resident Regiment was still out on exercise.

The Territorials were expected to vacate before they returned so as not to promote any animosity. They had already voiced their thoughts about accommodating them when they refused them the use of the armoury. After lunch the guys boarded coaches to take them to Brunswick for the night, much to the chagrin of the senior ranks who had to attend a Mess function and The Commissioned Officers who were to be hosted by the local Burgers.

It was deemed prudent to let the guys loose in the much larger city of Brunswick instead of the smaller and quieter town of Wolfenbuttel. The resident German and British garrisons were tolerated but they would not appreciate the appearance of 100 odd Yeomen with a "Brits on tour" mentality. The coaches dropped them outside the Schloss in the main square with warnings to be back there by midnight. "Yeah, right" seemed to be the scornful reply of most of them.

Although they started off in Troop groups, these broke down as mates sought out each other and those with similar character traits banded together. Some decided to head for something to eat whilst others headed straight to the red light area of The Bruchstrasse with its offer of family shows, topless bars, brothels and pubs which catered for all tastes.

Every town in Germany had a red light district. In the case of Brunswick it was The Bruchstrasse. A single street of old, multi-story wooden framed buildings which housed sex shops, pubs and brothels and was screened from view at both ends of the street by a wall. The locals knew it was there and policy was that if it offended, you didn't go there. Prostitution was legal in Germany but only on licenced premises. The state took its share of revenue in the form of taxes from the establishments, the workers being expected to declare their earnings and show evidence that they were medically "clean".

The attitude to the experience by the members of Pete's group was pretty typical. The young kids for who it was a new experience, egged on by the supposedly "old hands" had to prove themselves. Others, disenchanted with their own married situations saw it as a chance for some casual sex with no comeback. Pete had been with prostitutes twice before and had found both experiences to be a disappointment. He was happy to have a drink in a bar, preferably a Belgian Beer, served by a topless waitress and watch the dirty film being screened on the wall.

The visits to the various bars was interlaced with those to the sex shows which all had a similar format. For a fixed price you were allowed one drink of your choice and to watch the show which varied in content and quality. You had to buy further drinks though to continue watching, at an extortionate price. The secret was to catch a decent show, get value for money and then leave. Pete was watching with pleasure the young kids, who because of their naivety were being fleeced by the near naked waitresses. They would sidle up to the obviously pissed victim, sit on his knee and start fondling them. The idiots, being flattered, would be coaxed into buying them a drink, usually champagne for which they would be charged an insane amount. It would of course just be lemonade. If there was any trouble, they were kicked out on their arse. As the night went on the kids inevitably started buying girls and Pete's protective instincts took over. He convinced them to only take the price of the trick in with them and leave the rest of their money safe with him. The chances are that they would get rolled, be beaten, robbed and dumped in an alley somewhere.

The novelty for Pete, soon wore off though and he wandered off on his own, deciding that he had stayed with the group long enough for them not to think him a miserable bastard. Walking out of Bruchstrasse by the southern gate, he bought some Thai street food before catching a taxi on the Kalenwall. This took him over the medieval defensive canal south to the suburb of Gartenstadt.

Inevitably, the coaches that left at midnight had a few less passengers.

The majority of them showed up in small groups throughout the night, having been charged a fortune by Turkish taxi drivers.

Pete was dropped off the next morning by a woman who was distinctly older than himself but was athletic in build and had a military aura about her. Charlie, who had duties at the guardhouse watched them and was once again intrigued by Cpl Wood. He crossed over the entrance road and entered the medical centre opposite. Having signed for the two "Dickheads" who had been arrested during the night, he now had to find another one who had been admitted after falling down the coach steps. He had been awarded the duty of "Officer of the day" by The Squadron Leader as punishment for falling asleep at the dinner party hosted by the local dignitaries the night before.

At breakfast, there was a lot of very sick soldiers who were not looking forward to the long journey home. Most of them just wanted to go to sleep or simply curl up in a ball and die. Following a parade, The Squadron boarded coaches for the journey to Hannover Airport where they began the ball ache of the return journey home. Before boarding the flight they were paraded in front of a customs officer who asked them if they had anything to declare. As a Squadron they replied "No Sir" and he noted that they were all carrying the same striped paper bags which were associated with the sex shops of Germany. They were no doubt full of illegal publications and videos as were the thousands of others he had seen over the last two weeks. It wasn't worth the trouble he reasoned and mentally tried to recall the list of items his colleagues back in The UK had requested of him.

The land element of The Squadron, consisting of ADMIN and the LAD had left Warendorf on the Friday and travelled to The Hook of Holland for an overnight ferry crossing to Hull. A Townsend Thorenson vessel had been requisitioned for the job and carried the whole of The Regimental land party and that of a sister Regiment. Although many of them had been pissed at not getting a night in Brunswick, the crossing soon developed into a "party cruise". A Regimental

Police section was formed to ensure discipline on the boat but it soon became clear that they were going to be ineffective. As the night wore on the crowd evolved into 3 distinct groups. In the middle were the English contingents of the two Regiments. At one end of the boat were members of one Squadron which recruited from Scotland and at the other end, members of a Squadron who recruited in Northern Ireland. Trouble was expected as the two Celtic groups started to compete, attempting to out sing each other which then turned to cajoling. Then the pipes appeared, being played first in competition and eventually in unison.

The English were unaware that this was a common ritual carried out by the rival pipers of Scotland and Northern Ireland. They often travelled over the sea to compete with each other, in many cases they were cousins and the Red Hand of Ulster was sin ominous with the livery of Glasgow Rangers.

As the night continued, the English slowly relaxed and a good time was had by all.

Arriving back at the drill hall a full day ahead of the air party, they returned the weapons to the armoury and the myriad of items to the stores. The SQMS, as the senior soldier present, consented to them going home on the stipulation that they all return the next day. For most of them, particularly the guard detail, this went without question as they all wanted to be there when the Squadron bar was opened.

The next day, they **were** all there when the air party arrived. The return of the personal G10 equipment was carried out as quickly as possible as was the necessary official documentation of returning I.D. cards and dog tags. As the Squadron Leader finished his speech about the achievements and professionalism shown by them all he also thanked them and asked that they, in turn, thank their wives and loved one without whose support, The Squadron could not function.

The opening of the squadron bar was a noisy affair and the guys all saw it differently. To some it was the end of another training year and others saw it as the beginning of the next. Some were glad it was over and looked forward to a return to reality and their families. Some were sorry that it was over and were deflated at the thoughts of returning to work and the 9 to 5. There was always a few who swore to themselves that this would be their last exercise. Some of them would leave but the majority would carry on.

In reality, it was a continuous cycle of activity which never ended. The following weekend would involve the cleaning and maintenance of all the weapons and the return of G10 to the stores. Q would have to arrange for the sleeping bags and liners to be sent away for fumigation and professional cleaning as well as indenting for those items that had been lost or damaged. Over the following weeks, the vehicles would have to be collected from the container depot, de-kitted and then serviced before the training year began all over again.

As the bar slowly emptied during the course of the night, Charlie knew that he had one more duty to fulfil before he could return to his family. One of his Troop was unaccounted for and he saw it as his responsibility to check on the welfare of Smudger.

GLOSSARY

A.A.C.	Army Air Corps
A10	American Ground Attack Aircraft
ADMIN	Logistical Support Troop
AK 47	Russian assault rifle
B.A.O.R	British Army of the Rhine
BATUS	British Army Training Unit Suffield
BEASTING	Verbal or physical abuse
BIVVY	Shelter or tent
BLITZKRIEG	Aggressive form of air and ground assault
BLOWPIPE	Shoulder fired anti- aircraft missile
BMH	British Military Hospital
BO 105	German Light Observation Helicopter
BOVVY	Bovington, Armoured Training establishment
BOX HEAD	Square head / German
BRIGADE	Sub unit of a Division
BRIXMIS	British Military Mission
BTR 70	Russian wheeled armoured personnel carrier
BUNDESWEHR	West German Army
CHARLIE G	Carl Gustav anti-tank weapon
CHIEFTAIN	British main battle tank
CORNET	Alternative term for a 2nd Lieutenant
CV	Command vehicle
CVR(T)	Combat vehicle reconnaissance (tracked)
CVR(W)	Combat vehicle reconnaissance (wheeled)
DIXIE	Cooking vessel

EGG BANGO	Fried egg sandwich
FELDWEBEL	German equivalent to Sergeant
FOX	British armoured reconnaissance vehicle
FROGFOOT	Russian ground attack aircraft
FTX	Field training exercise
FUCHS	German armoured reconnaissance vehicle
G.P.M.G	General Purpose Machine Gun
G10	An issued item of equipment or clothing
GAT	Nickname for the Sub Machine Gun
GEFREITER	German äquivalent to Corporal
HERDIE FERDIE	Herforder Pils (German lager)
JAGERPANZER IV	German WWII tank destroyer
JAGUAR	German armoured anti-tank missile vehicle
JIMPY	Nickname for the G.P.M.G
L.A.D.	Light aid detachment (Recovery and repair)
LAW	Light anti-tank weapon
LMG	Light machine gun
LUCHS	German wheeled reconnaissance vehicle
LUFTWAFFE	German Air Force
M.O.D.	Ministry of Defence
M2	Mobile bridging system
MARDER	German tracked A.P.C.
MAW	Medium anti-tank weapon
MLRS	Multi launch rocket system
MONKEY	Nick name for a British Military Policeman
MSR	Main supply route
N.C.O	Non-commissioned officer

NBC	Nuclear biological and chemical
O GROUP	Orders group
O.P.	Observation post
P.S.I.	Permanent staff instructor
PHANTOM	Fighter/ground attack aircraft
POL	Petrol, oil and lubricants
PUMA	Utility and transport helicopter
PYRO	Pyrotechnics
Q	Abbreviation of Quartermaster
RAF	Royal Air Force
RAF REGIMENT	Royal Air Force ground defence force
RARDEN	30mm Automatic cannon
REGIMENT	The sub unit of a Brigade
REPLEN	Replenish
RHQ	Regimental headquarters
RPG	Rocket powered grenade
RV	Rendez-vous point
S.O.P.	Standing operating procedure
S.S.M	Squadron Sergeant Major
SABRE TROOP	Armoured reconnaissance troop
SAMARITAN	Tracked armoured ambulance
SAMSON	Tracked armoured recovery vehicle
SAS	Special Air Service
SCORPION	Tracked armoured reconnaissance vehicle
SCOUT	Observation and liaison helicopter
SEA STALLION	German utility and transport helicopter
SECTION	Sub unit of a platoon or troop

SHELLREP	Report of an artillery strike
SHQ	Squadron headquarters
SLR	Self-loading rifle
SMG	Sub machine gun
SOXMIS	Soviet diplomatic mission
SPANDAU	German general purpose machine gun
SPARTAN	Tracked armoured personnel carrier
SQUADRON	Sub unit of an Armoured Regiment
STAG	Slang for tour of duty
SULTAN	Tracked armoured command vehicle
THUNDERFLASH	A simulated grenade pyrotechnic
TOC. H	A shop supplying sundries to soldiers
TORNADO	Western Fighter / Ground Attack aircraft
TOW	Anti-tank missile system
TRACKED RAPIER	Mobile air defence system
TROOP	Sub unit of a Squadron
TROOP LEADER	Officer commanding a Troop
VC10	Airliner used by The Royal Air Force
VCP	Vehicle check point
VOLKSTURM	German home guard
WAFFEN SS	Military arm of The SS
WARRIOR	Tracked armoured personnel carrier
WEASEL	German light tracked assault vehicle
WESSEX	British transport helicopter
WHITE MICE	British mobile operational security unit

Printed in Great Britain
by Amazon

80817472R00108